I0594055

# Feathergill's Fabulous Emporium

*Where You Wear Your Words*

Written & Illustrated
by
Mary Coons

Sir Wallace

Lady Lydia

Mariah

Susan

Cook

Wesley

Phineas Peabody

Charlotte

Hepzibah

Abigail Sprocklebott    June Mooney    Mrs. Stabberback

Letitia Short    Dr. Brown    Henry Greene

Rosé Greene    Mrs Lapsis    Prof. Longley

Name: Mary Coons
Title: Feathergill's Fabulous Emporium: Where You Wear Your Words
Written & Illustrated by Mary Coons
Cover Design: Mary Coons
ISBN: 978-0-9769179-2-2
LCCN:  2021919424
Subjects: 1. Young Adult/Fiction/Visionary & Metaphysical
2. Young Adult/Fiction/Literary
3. Young Adult/Fantasy/Historical


Published by
North Pine Publications
Indianapolis, Indiana

# Also by the Author

The Piglys and the Hundred-Year Mystery

The Storysaurus Book: How To Tell a Round Story

The Art of Noticing

*Dedicated to the fellowship of the orphaned heart.*

*You know who you are.*

# CHAPTER ONE

*The Hawthorn*

"Elizabeth? Are you up there?"

"Yes."

Paulina looked through branches of the old hawthorn to see Elizabeth, nestled in the crook of two upper limbs. Hawthorn trees, covered with thorny spikes, are impossible to climb. But this hawthorn, only this one, recognized a girl who needed to escape the drudgery of daily life at St. Gumbert's Orphan Asylum, and for such girls, the spikes curled into little balls, useful as climbing handholds.

Paulina and Elizabeth were two such girls.

Paulina stepped onto a low branch. Elizabeth, perched much higher, tore her gaze from the gypsy camp beyond the orphanage wall. She had spent the afternoon watching the horses, goats, and chickens in the camp sprawled haphazardly in the east meadow, admiring the painted wagons that served as gypsy homes. Her eyes drank in colorful, piecemeal clothing, her ears were tuned to accordion music. The smell of good things cooking in a big black pot reached her nose when the wind was right.

Looking down, she saw Paulina's distressed face.

"'Lizabeth—did you see the motorcar coming up the drive just now?"

"Yes." The sight of a motorcar, *any* motorcar, was very interesting at the time of this story, about 1910.

"That was Simon Suggs driving. Simon Suggs – with that awful garment factory, where Matron sends us when we're through here. Listen, 'Lizabeth—stay out of his sight, whatever you do. You're almost ten, and, well, better safe than sorry.

"Oh! And Cook wants you in the kitchen. Myra the maid quit, and Cook is fit to be tied. So she needs you. Matron wants to meet with me, but

I'm sure I'll be back after supper. What a bother, but we all sweep when Matron hands out brooms, don't we? Anyway, 'Lizabeth, a storm's coming - you can't stay out."

Elizabeth sighed, and reluctantly worked her way down from her perch. She had been climbing the hawthorn since she was four years old, and she knew the various pleasures the branches held — the peace to read a book, the comfort of pulling her baby ring from its safe place beneath her uniform and rubbing her thumb across the patterned surface. She considered herself too old for make-believe, but still, she liked to pretend the gold ring - her only token of her real parents — was like a magic lamp, able to take her to a real home.

The hawthorn's best treat, though, was the view: farms, fields, houses — other people's homes. Even movable homes, like the gypsy camp. The sight gave hope that some day, some how, she would have one of her own. She was sorry to have her afternoon cut short.

Elizabeth jumped off one of the lower limbs, but the branch below, as if anxious to hold her, caught her skirt, and she heard it tear. Oh, no! A ripped uniform meant certain punishment unless she could get the mending done before Matron saw. She'd have to be quick, and skillful, which she could manage, but still, she worried, just as she worried at the possibility of losing Paulina. If Paulina wanted *her* to hide from Simon Suggs, what about Paulina, who was nearly sixteen? She was the best and brightest of the girls at St. Gumbert's. Orphans went away when they turned sixteen. Elizabeth frowned. She pinched the torn uniform skirt together and made her way toward the scullery door.

The uniforms at St. Gumbert's Orphan Asylum had, apparently, been designed by some demented scientist, Elizabeth had always thought. They contrived to be hot in summer, cold in winter, and their prickly fabric caused discomfort all year round. They ripped easily, because they were made at Suggs Utility Garment factory of spun thistle fiber, the cheapest material found anywhere. Yellowish gray in color, they looked good on not one of St. Gumbert's fifty orphaned girls. Fair girls looked pale and sickly; they made Elizabeth, with brown hair and eyes, look bilious, as if she were seasick. They poked and caused rashes at the waist and armpits; they were as stiff as celery when new, but by the end of a year's wear, devolved into being sullen, limp, and decrepit like a constantly complaining invalid nursed through a tiresome illness.

Uniforms, by Asylum policy, had to last the year. Matron's watchword was "thrift." Cook, her round bulk wrapped in an apron that had once been white, and seated on her favorite red stool, cast an appraising eye at Elizabeth's ripped skirt.

"You'd best be mending that before Matron gets a glimpse of what you've done, girl. You do NOT want to face her at End-of-Day with a torn uniform."

More will be said about End-of-Day later.

"I suppose you'd better do it now, 'cause there won't be time after dinner." Cook sighed heavily. "But hurry, Lizzie, 'cause I do need the help. Myra's gone and quit, Paulina's off with Matron, and there's nobody to stir the stew."

Elizabeth hurried into the old butler's pantry where she had a secret place for treasures like her sewing kit. At St. Gumbert's, no orphan could count on keeping nice things unless she devised a place to ferret them away.

More will be said about Elizabeth's secret place, later.

She got out needle and thread and whipstitched furiously, pushing back the short strands of hair that mutinied from their place behind her ear.

"Hurry through with that fix, Lizzie, the stew is sticking to the pot!" But Elizabeth paused. She heard crying from the other side of the pantry wall. That would be the orphanage office. Then she heard Matron's voice. You couldn't mistake the sound, very much like the *caw, caw* of a displeased crow.

"They all cry when they first come, but they settle in. We'll make a place for her, with your contribution to our Orphan Fund."

"Lizzie!" Cook called from the kitchen, and Elizabeth cut and knotted her thread, straightened her skirt, and went to stir the stew.

Years earlier, Cook had enlisted Elizabeth as her kitchen helper. She learned to mix and stir and pour and chop, to read recipes and deal with cantankerous tradesmen. She became adept at keeping a straight face when she needed to keep a secret, which was often, and at getting around Asylum rules, which changed with the whim of Matron.

*Matron! The trouble comes back to Matron,* Elizabeth thought as she tried to keep her nose away from the smell of Cook's supper concoction—something not quite fresh in the pot, she assessed. Cutting corners and keeping secrets and making do were part of life because of Matron. She made things *difficult.* The orphans had to be quiet, or get in trouble. They

4

had to get to meals on time and needed to appear to be working when they were assigned to work, or Matron's face would turn red, her voice, unpleasant at the best of times, would become a screech, and the fly swatter she always had at hand would be employed on the orphan who had transgressed. Elizabeth was fortunate, she supposed, to be separate from the schedule and most of the rules.

She turned her attention to stirring.

The evening was bleak. As Paulina had foreseen, a storm had blown through, leaving the yard a sea of mud. The orphans were hungry – dinner had been a stew of ingredients no one could identify, not even Elizabeth, who had done the stirring, and the rolls alongside were moldy. Simon Suggs was nowhere to be seen, but neither was Paulina. Elizabeth helped clean up the kitchen, wondering all the while: *where was she?* Paulina was the anchor in her life. *Where can she be?* Elizabeth thought, as she trudged her weary way to bed.

The path to the orphans' wing was a journey of ever-diminishing elegance. From the foyer with marble pillars, statuary and flocked wallpaper, a massive marble staircase rose to a gilded hallway running past a series of fancy carved doors on one side, a dizzying view of the grand entry hall on the other. At the hallway's end, the traveler was forced to turn left in order to avoid a rather damp alcove reserved for unwanted furniture. The narrow door led to a long, dim hallway, where another narrow door on the right admitted the visitor to what had once been the loft over the stables. As Elizabeth ducked through the entrance, a hand touched her shoulder. She spun around. Paulina pulled her back into the alcove and whispered, "'Lizabeth! Pay close attention, and don't ask questions.

"I want you to take care of the new girl. I know you can; you're the only one. I won't be here." Paulina bit her lower lip and scrunched up her eyes. "I'll be gone, just for a while. I'm trusting you. Goodbye, dear." She ended this speech with a quick, hard, hug, then grabbed a satchel and ran down the hall. Elizabeth watched her get smaller and smaller in the distance.

Inside the long, narrow dormitory, cots had been moved away from leaky windows after the storm. Since the room had once been the attic over the stables, and had sloped eaves on either side, you could only stand up straight in the middle. With cots scrunched away from the walls, navigation was difficult.

Elizabeth's cot was jammed beside the door, an arrangement that allowed her to get out early for work in the kitchen. She sat down and scanned the orphans scurrying and tripping around to wash and change before bedtime. In the middle of the room, in the middle of a tiny cot, sat a small yellow-haired girl, crying. In the next bed a girl Elizabeth disliked followed her gaze and remarked, "Mind your own business, Lizzie. She'll get used to things. One good thing—Warden and Matron have to go to making arrangements, so there's no End-of-Day tonight."

Elizabeth picked her way over to the newcomer and knelt beside her.

"What's your name?" she whispered.

"Shah-wott."

Elizabeth paused, considered, and asked, "Char-lotte?"

The new orphan nodded, and repeated, "Shah-wott, and I want my mama!"

"Don't we all!" sniped the girl in the next bed. "The sooner you learn you don't *have* a mama, the better for you!"

Elizabeth ignored her and took a good look at the new girl. Perhaps three or four years old, too little to pronounce her own name, and left on her own in the cold, bleak, orphan dormitory. Soft blond curls, round blue-green eyes, lashes that stopped just short of curling into complete circles, dimpled cheeks tinted pink and more dimples at her knees and elbows. She

6

looked like a china doll and smelled of a perfumed soap Elizabeth did not recognize, although she could say with certainty it had never been used at St. Gumbert's. This, then, was the girl Paulina meant. She gathered Charlotte and her blankets up in her arms.

"I've got you. We'll share my cot tonight, till you feel at home."

"I'm telling!" said the other orphan, at whom Elizabeth directed a nasty look.

Charlotte wiped her eyes with the back of her hand and settled her head into the crook of Elizabeth's shoulder. Elizabeth made her way to her own cot.

She covered the newcomer, then crawled under the blanket and fell asleep wondering how, or when, anyone would feel at home at the Asylum.

# CHAPTER TWO

*St. Gumbert's Orphan Asylum*

Many an orphan had spent many a long day at St. Gumbert's in its thirty-year history, but we only have one, set to be Elizabeth's last. The reader may want to know what orphan life was like, so we'll provide a description.

Generally speaking, the days were framed by an odd mixture of arbitrary rules and perilously lax practices, for the daily schedule was designed for the convenience of Matron. In the mornings, after a breakfast of lumpy oatmeal or thin porridge, the orphans, except Elizabeth, were herded out of Matron's way and into the Asylum schoolroom. Once used as the stable, the long, narrow space squatted directly under the dormitory we described earlier, if the reader remembers. Never intended for people, the room was drafty and damp. Horses had once been needed to take guests to parties and dinners and church. But nowadays, none of the orphans went anywhere, so horses were sold, and the stables made into a classroom, where long tables served as desks, and benches for seats. The schoolmistress, overwhelmed, overworked, and seldom paid, took no attendance and was secretly thankful for absentees. Orphans got just enough schooling so they could, when sent out into the world, read instructions left by the ladies for whom they would be maids and servants.

Elizabeth was different; she spent her mornings in the kitchen. Years before, Cook had noticed she picked up reading and arithmetic like a carpet sweeper picks up breadcrumbs, so she made her a helper in the big black-and-white tiled kitchen, where her ability to read recipes was especially useful. Cook reigned as queen from a red stool in the middle of the room, surrounded by a panoply of pots and pans hung from hooks on the walls the way shields and swords used to hang in the halls of ancient kings. In one corner, a clean marble counter was set aside for the chef who came in twice a week to prepare delicacies for Matron. That was the kitchen.

We're on a mission to describe the schedule at St. Gumbert's, but, as we will soon be leaving, we must also take time to describe the rest of the house. It will be important, later in the adventure.

The reader already knows about the block wall around the orphanage, so the reader might think St. Gumbert's resembled a prison. The spiked wall, with a frowning gatehouse like an ugly pendant on a thorny chain, would certainly leave that impression. Actually, the wall was a late addition built ten years earlier on instructions from Matron. Within the wall, the house was more like a captive castle. Three stories of pink granite, festooned with turrets and gables, still sat gracefully amongst overgrown shrubs. Many-paned windows placed everywhere the architect could adroitly fit them glittered in the sun wherever they hadn't been boarded up. A century earlier, the granite had had a pearly glow when touched by sun or moonlight, but now was covered with dead vines and splotches of debris and dirt. The lawns had turned to weed patches after years of neglect. A fountain, once the lawn's crown jewel, sat broken and dry.

Inside, the best rooms went unused. On the first floor, Matron's cluttered quarters could be reached by anyone brave enough to navigate the narrow passage that snaked alongside the main staircase. Also on the main floor were a series of fabulous formal salons serving no useful purpose except keeping orphans busy dusting and polishing. Up the sweeping marble stairway, a visitor would find, behind those fancy doors, sumptuous bedchambers, unoccupied. The stable wing branched off toward the backyard and was the orphans' quarters, as we've already mentioned.

Another flight of stairs led to the third floor, which Matron kept locked. She never said why.

Under the kitchen, in the cellar, was the Punishment Room, where rats were the only regular occupants. More will be said about the Punishment Room, later.

St. Gumbert's was a big place, and that brings us back to the schedule. For in the afternoons, the orphans were put to work scrubbing and polishing the places a visitor might see — those fancy chambers on the first floor, especially. Their own rooms received a slapdash lick-and-a-promise if time remained after everything else was as spotless as harried and underfed orphans could be forced to make it.

Morning or afternoon, St. Gumbert's schedule included no time for play. The more adventurous orphans contrived ways around this, sliding down banisters, skating on wet floors, indulging in hide-and-seek behind statuary they were supposed to be scrubbing. Of course, they got in

10

trouble when they were caught, but they reckoned a little bit of fun was worth the punishment. Besides, with St. Gumbert's scanty staff, they were not found out so often as you might expect.

Elizabeth worked and studied by herself, with special instruction from Paulina. After helping Cook tidy up the midday meal, she was supposed to get special lessons from Nancy, the schoolmistress, but Nancy usually sent her to the library, where Paulina managed the books. Which was fine with Elizabeth.

We forgot to mention the library, which was silly of us, since it was Elizabeth's favorite room. The door was on the second floor, but the room extended two stories up to a wonderful stained-glass skylight. Surrounded by books and snuggled into one of the old leather chairs, she could pretend to be a princess or an explorer or an artist, and she did. After a while, the atmosphere and Paulina's encouragement had worked on her mind, and she took up the study of what she found. Starting with the fairy tales on the bottom shelves, she had read her way up to the histories, biographies, science, and mathematics on the shelves higher and higher up. Paulina had been quick to help and answer questions. In this manner, Elizabeth had acquired a wide, if spotty, body of knowledge, almost an education.

The other orphans mocked her manners and her bookishness whenever they got the chance. The saving grace was Paulina, who had eyes to see character and determination and intelligence in Elizabeth. She told her stories of olden days and better times at the orphanage, shared treats and blankets and books, took the place of a big sister. But when orphans turned sixteen, they were sent out to make their way in the world. *Was Paulina gone for good?*

There were other rooms that we haven't mentioned, but that will have to do for now. For a stressful and momentous day is brewing at St. Gumbert's Orphan Asylum, down between the kitchen and dining room.

# CHAPTER THREE

## A Mysterious Package

Next morning, Elizabeth got up to embark on what was to be her last day at St. Gumbert's, although, as we mentioned, she did not know it. She left Charlotte asleep and slipped downstairs. Pushing open the swinging kitchen door, she stepped aside to let in Grimalkin, the orphanage cat. *Probably going upstairs to her kittens*, Elizabeth surmised while trying her best to ignore the mouse being carried by the tail. Slipping her apron over her head, she moved a stepstool in front of the stove, and set to work stirring a large vat of oatmeal. Then she heard the tradesman's bell at the back gate.

"You get that, Lizzie. I'm all tied up getting the liver ready for lunch," said Cook, who avoided any movement that didn't result immediately in a snack or a nap. She handed over a cumbersome key. Elizabeth stepped out into the yard, picked a careful path around mud puddles and a few of the orphanage chickens, and used the key to open the iron gate in the gray block wall.

And there, in the morning light, she saw a postman in a blue uniform, on a bicycle.

"I have a package for a young lady named Charlotte," he said, and handed Elizabeth a brown paper package, tied with soft string and smelling of lavender. It made a fresh, crinkly sound in her outstretched hands.

"But mail goes to the front gate, sir," she said.

"But *you*, my dear, are at the back gate." And the postman smiled, tipped his cap, and pedaled away. As she watched the departing bicycle, she could have sworn she saw wings—silvery, nearly transparent wings— on the back of its rider. She blinked and rubbed her eyes, but the winged postman had disappeared, and she was left to ponder the package and the mystery of its delivery.

His enigmatic remark stayed with her. *She* had the package, which normally would have gone straight from the mailbox to Matron's desk from where, Elizabeth knew from experience, it would never get to Charlotte. Items mailed to orphans were confiscated upon arrival at St. Gumbert's.

She looked at the address, one word, in flowing script, with flourishes: *Charlotte*. Then, at the return address: *Feathergill's Emporium, Granger's Green.* Elizabeth had heard of Granger's Green—a small town, away across the hills, east of the orphanage, far beyond her experience.

She slipped the package between her uniform and her petticoat, then re-tied her apron to hold it snug. The secret would need to be carefully guarded if it were ever to get to Charlotte. Elizabeth worried about the noise the wrapping made when she moved. She felt a glow of curiosity, what on earth could the package contain? Her heart was warmed by the trust placed in her by the mysterious mailman.

These thoughts took no more time than it took to secure the parcel. She patted her waist, straightened the uniform, and was just about to turn back. But before she stepped inside the gray walls, she looked across the fields and saw the sunrise had become a wild swirl of purples and pinks, streaked with orange. A flock of swallows flew across the sky. Set against the sunrise, their outlines were as sharp as knives, exquisitely detailed. *They can go anywhere they want*, thought Elizabeth. *Even home.*

Taking a deep breath, she opened the gate and returned to the oatmeal.

# CHAPTER FOUR

### *Two Dinners*

On this particular day, Elizabeth hoped to get away from the kitchen early to check on Charlotte. Sometimes that was possible. She started to slip out of her apron when the oatmeal was done.

"Not so fast, Lizzie," Cook called out. "Today's a day I needs you in the kitchen. You can start chopping me some carrots whiles you eat your breakfast." Elizabeth had to stay put.

Matron was expecting important visitors for dinner, and Cook was in a frenzy. A visiting chef with a snooty attitude arrived mid-morning and took charge of the menu and the kitchen. Having to do her own job and, at the same time, be at his beck and call did not sit well with Cook. Instead of her usual afternoon routine of napping or reading novels, she shouted orders and commands to Elizabeth at five-minute intervals as the morning ended and the afternoon rolled on. Delicacies and dainties the orphans had never seen were planned, and roasts needed basting, soups needed stirring, egg whites needed to be carefully whipped into meringues. Elizabeth was busy every minute, obeying conflicting orders from a grumpy Cook and the grumpier chef. Normally, Paulina would have been there to lighten the load of the work and the mood of the workers, but Paulina was nowhere to be seen. Elizabeth looked up hopefully every time the door swung open, but her friend never appeared. Charlotte's mysterious package stayed secure, held next to her heart, but she couldn't deliver it. She felt tied to the kitchen by her apron strings.

Her last task was to help Dorrie, the housemaid, lay the china, silver, and cut-glass for the banquet on the table that stretched like a highway down the middle of the formal dining room. Elizabeth liked Dorrie. She said she only "obliged" as a maid because her fiancé, Tony, lived in the gypsy camp, and her mother lived nearby. She could easily find a better job elsewhere, she said. Since staff at the Asylum changed more often than the sheets on their beds, Elizabeth's fondness was mixed with caution—maids she liked usually left.

But in this case, she felt nothing but delight to see Dorrie and her curly red hair because Charlotte was tagging behind, holding the hem of her apron with a chubby hand. *If she's with Dorrie, she's safe*, thought Elizabeth.

She helped set out the dinner forks, the salad forks, the fish forks, the soup spoons and tea spoons and dessert spoons, the dinner knives and steak knives, all in their proper places, and then the dinner plates and soup plates and water goblets and wine glasses, then the artfully folded napkins and mathematically positioned butter knives and salt dishes.

Dorrie usually moved with the speed of rushing water through any task she undertook, but today her progress was slow. She paused two or three times with a spoon in her hand. A frown creased her pretty forehead.

"I kept this little mite with me, all day. Paulina was supposed to do it, but Matron called her away. What Matron's thinking, taking in a tiny one— I can't imagine. How's she going to put a baby to work here? How's she going to fit into school here? If you ask me, it's just plain wrong." Dorrie twisted a strand of her red hair around her finger, something she did when she was worried. "Well, never mind, and let's finish the table setting." But she kept talking as she put tall tapers in the candlesticks. "Matron only takes 'em in if they're old enough to do jobs, and that I know for sure and certain. She's hardly got any maids but me and Janet, for she's got you girls doing all the work!" Dorrie sniffed. "Downright sinful, IF you ask me, which of course no one does, or I'd tell 'em." She paused, then continued, "Matron's mean, and she's weak. That's a bad combination. And oh, my! is she in a temper today. The Asylum Board of Bigwigs is due for dinner,

16

along with that awful little man who runs Suggs's Utility Garments, and she does not know HOW to be in a worse mood than she's already in."

"Tell me about Suggs's Utility Garments," Elizabeth said, setting down a knife, and thinking back to Paulina.

Dorrie became uncharacteristically quiet. "Well, never you mind. Not fit to talk about, is Suggs's, and certainly not a place you have to worry about, at least not for a while. But tonight, Simon Suggs is here for dinner, and he's bringing his sister, which is just worse."

By now the table was set, except for place cards. Elizabeth handled the one to be placed at Matron's right hand. "Malice Suggs," she read. "Muh-leese?" she questioned. "Suggs?"

Dorrie giggled. "No, *Malice*. Rhymes with *Alice*. It's Miss Suggs's first name. Maybe her name is why she is the way she is, and maybe she's the reason he is the way he is, I don't know. But whatever the reason, that pair of Suggses is like a nightmare come to visit."

She straightened her apron and took Charlotte by the hand that wasn't being used for thumb-sucking. "Come with me, biddie—I've got some good supper." They stepped into the servants' hall, just off the kitchen. The walls were lined with shelves of spice tins, jars of jellies and preserves. A solid table stood in the middle where the hired help ate. Dorrie found an old biscuit tin, topped it with clean dishtowels, and put the resulting arrangement on a chair for Charlotte. She finished her monologue with a flourish of a dishtowel.

"I don't like Matron inviting the Suggses, indeed I don't. Cook says nothing's been the same since she made friends with them. She says it's been a bad eleven years. And, I don't mind telling you, their factory is a house of horrors. My cousin worked there once. She got away, but not many girls do. Girls work long, hot hours in front of nasty machines with sharp needles and scratchy fabrics, six and a half days of every week. Simon Suggs is always looking to make it bigger, make it make him more money,

17

so he and that sister of his make the girls who work there work till they drop. Suggs Utility Garments makes piles of uniforms, aprons, and overalls. Abbreviated S.U.G.—get it? Sorta' spells his name. Simon Suggs likes everything to be about *him*. And the fabric! Spun thistle fiber, stiff and sticky as gummed pipe cleaners, and cheap as cheap can be. Well, you know—you're wearing one. They're awful."

She busied herself dividing a loaf of fresh brown bread and a waxed block of firm yellow cheese into portions and gave one to Charlotte, another to Elizabeth.

"Supper for orphans tonight is leftover sour-beet-stew," said Dorrie, scrunching up her delicate nose. "I surely don't see how anyone gets it down, but handily, I've got some good bread and cheese to share." She took a deep breath. "I've kept this little new-bie all day, and she's been talking about her mama. Funny thing, though—she gets real quiet when I give her some paper and a pencil. Sets down and draws pictures, nice as pie. What do you make of that?" Staff at St. Gumbert's talked to Elizabeth like she was one of them.

"I don't know, Dorrie."

Dorrie stared at the wall. Then she straightened her shoulders and shook her head. "I don't know what's gotten into me—can't seem to keep my mind on my work." Then her eyes fell on the package, which Elizabeth had just managed to extract from under her apron.

"What do you have there, Miss Elizabeth?" she asked. "Look at that beautiful penmanship! I wonder what *Feathergill's* is."

The mystery of the package was scarcely solved by opening. The wrapping paper, untied and unfolded, revealed tissue paper. The tissue paper, a silvery gray color, felt crisp and silky at the same time. When that was folded back, a whiff of lavender greeted them. They saw a lace collar with tiny pearl buttons for fastening, and a letter "C" worked into the lace.

The letter stood out against a sash of deep blue green. Charlotte touched the sash with one chubby finger. The color matched her eyes.

"Where did these come from, and what do they mean?" Elizabeth asked.

"Land-a-Goshen, what lace work and weaving! I've never seen the like, not even in the fancy shops in Gumbertville," said Dorrie.

Charlotte looked at Elizabeth. "These are for me? Thankyouvewwymuch…May I have a *dress* to go between the pieces, pwease?"

# CHAPTER FIVE

*Missing!*

The minutes before bedtime at St. Gumbert's were the worst of the day, and that was saying something. All fifty orphans washed themselves in cold water from basins, then lined up beside their beds for inspection. The two rows of cots under the eaves looked like train tracks running into the distance from Elizabeth's bed next to the door.

Matron looked over each girl, and then read, not a bedtime story—oh, no!—but a list of things done wrong that day, and by whom. That was the End-of-Day we mentioned earlier. When a girl was singled out for a mistake, she received a scolding, or a spanking, or, horror of horrors, a night in the Punishment Room, about which more will be said later, as promised.

Tonight, the orphans had been warned to be on their best behavior, for the orphanage's Governing Board, as well as the Suggses, were coming up with Matron for the End-of-Day. Elizabeth felt curious—she seldom saw anyone besides St. Gumbert's orphans and St. Gumbert's staff. Today, she thought, had begun with the mysterious postman and would end with these foreign dignitaries.

Matron's gray hair, styled up in a pompadour, competed with her chin, nose, and forehead to be the first part of her to enter a room. She marched through the door wearing the purple brocade she reserved for Occasions of Great Importance. A crystal bead fringe looked like icicles and rattled in the doorway. The dress sported mysterious side panels of a brighter shade of purple like misplaced stripes—Dorrie once told Elizabeth that Matron had let out the sides because she kept growing stouter, but wouldn't admit she needed a new gown.

Behind Matron, Elizabeth could see a clutter of bright colors set against shiny black. Then the clutter untangled and turned out to be a gaggle of six grownups in black dinner suits and bright silk gowns—the St. Gumbert's Orphan Asylum Board of Governors. The dresses were a feast for her eyes as they minced past, narrow stylish shapes in shades of slinky silk, bunched and ruched and gathered into short puffy sleeves, flounced peplums, and some rather odd draperies. To Elizabeth's fascination, long gloves snaked up their arms to collide with the sleeves. The women, taking tiny steps

21

because of extremely narrow skirts, formed a line, alternating with the men, in the middle of the room.

The gentlemen were less showy but just as interesting in their own way. Their mustache tips curled up in stiff circles, and one had a wedge-shaped beard that covered his necktie. Their dinner suits set off the pastel dresses and gave the impression of a mixed flock of crows and peacocks. They shuffled, looking embarrassed and awkward, as fifty pairs of orphan eyes stared.

So bright were the suits and dresses that Elizabeth almost didn't notice a small man in an orange checkered coat, sidling in behind. A bushy mustache sitting on his face failed to distract from his beady eyes and tiny chin. *This must be Simon Suggs,* she thought. His orange suit with narrow trousers stood out in front of a wide expanse of black satin that turned out to be his sister's dress. Elizabeth took a step backwards, the better to be out of his sight.

The orphans were scrubbed and nightgowned and ready, each beside her bed, but a problem presented itself in the middle of the room. Charlotte's place was empty. She was nowhere to be seen. Before anyone could concoct a story or hide her cot in a closet, the visitors had seen the empty space.

The girl who had threatened to tattle the night before, spoke now, "The new girl is gone! I bet *Elizabeth* knows where she is!"

She pursed her lips and looked prim. Matron glared at Elizabeth, who looked back steadfastly. If you flinched in the face of one of Matron's rages, you were done for, she knew, so she made herself stand up very straight. "No Ma'm, I don't."

Partly because of this, and partly because there were guests present, Matron reined herself in and did not fly into a rage. She poured her frustration into yanking the bell pull that hung by the door three times to summon the staff. Her crystal fringe tinkled as she waved her arms to

22

dispatch the housemaid, the schoolmistress, the groundskeeper, and even Cook, aroused from her after-supper nap, to search the house. The committee of Governors formed a circle, talking amongst themselves behind gloved hands, heads nodding like Cook's backdoor chickens. Skinny Mr. Suggs edged into their circle. His plump sister went and found a seat in the alcove.

The gentleman with the beard gave a nervous glance at Simon Suggs, then turned to Matron. "Madam. My esteemed colleagues and I," he said, "cannot help but think this is a severe failure. You cannot go about losing orphans!"

Matron's reply made matters worse, for she was no diplomat. Tapping her fan three times on the head of a nearby girl, she said, almost absent-mindedly, "Only one orphan, Mr. Ludlow, a very small one. New here, besides. She'll turn up somewhere. With fifty of them, a tight budget, and a limited staff, *I* can hardly be expected to keep track!"

The Board of Governors turned and bustled out. Matron continued to tap her fan on the gloved palm of her other hand. Then she, too, turned and walked into the hallway. The orphans were left alone.

Elizabeth bit her lip and thought. Nothing good would happen when Charlotte was found. End-of-Day punishments were bad enough for orphans accustomed to them, but would be awful for someone so little. Matron meted out consequences based on how much the infraction inconvenienced her, and this one, by that standard, was a whopper and would end with in a night in the Punishment Room, for sure. Elizabeth couldn't let herself think of a little girl — almost a baby — in there. With the rats.

We did promise, more than once, to describe the Punishment Room. Deep in the basement, under the kitchen, the dank chamber was part of a labyrinth of damp stone walls and brick arches that made up the orphanage cellars. Once, just once, Elizabeth had been there. When she was only five years old, she had, by accident, put a cup of salt instead of sugar into Matron's tea cake. Once had been enough to ensure she would never forget the moldy smell, the stone walls that seemed to be sweating some sort of slime, the rat skittering across the dirt floor to stare at her.

Then Cook had intervened. Elizabeth remembered the scraping sound of the key in the lock, the door opening, and Cook saying, gruffly, "Come along now. You'll do us no good down here, there's work to be done upstairs." And she had led her back to the kitchen. The single hour she had spent in the Punishment Room had filled many hours of nightmares since.

There are moments in all our lives that stand out from the rest, and, the moment Charlotte went missing would be one of Elizabeth's. A resolution formed in a place deep inside her, a moment of what is commonly called "making up her mind."

The other orphans chattered excitedly, and some had even started a pillow fight. No one noticed when she dropped down and gathered some things from the box under her bed, felt around her neck to make sure her baby ring was still secure on its chain, then grabbed the Feathergill's package from Charlotte's box. Concerned about the crispy, crinkly sound the paper made, she extracted the collar and sash and wrapped them up in her uniform. Then she tucked everything under her nightgown, slipped out the door, and made her way to the library down the hall.

It was evidence of the thinking at St. Gumbert's that no one thought to search the library. Tonight, her reason for heading there was different from her usual book-search. It was home to Grimalkin, a silver cat who had recently had five kittens. Alert readers will recall she was last seen carrying a dead mouse across the kitchen.

"Silver," as applied to any of the cats at St. Gumbert's, does not mean "a nice light blue-gray." It means, well, *silver*. Sparkly. The cats of St. Gumbert's had fur that actually glittered, and in the dark, glowed. Elizabeth had a good idea that the sight of Grimalkin's new silver kittens, now big

24

enough to explore the second floor, might have lured Charlotte away from the dormitory.

The immediate problem Elizabeth faced was getting around Malice Suggs, who had parked herself on a seat in the alcove and sat, very much resembling a toad on a log. Fortunately, as Elizabeth watched, Malice groaned and reached down to unhook the tiny buttons that fastened the top of her left shoe. Elizabeth heard her mutter, "Oh, my bunions!" She tiptoed past and slipped into the library.

There she found Grimalkin, her kittens, and Charlotte, curled up on a wide-seated library chair. Charlotte had a small pencil and a piece of paper with a drawing of a cat. The smallest kitten, the one with the white nose, was ensconced in Charlotte's lap, purring. Charlotte looked up.

"Liz-bet, look! I followed the kitty. I talked to the kitty. I DRAWED the kitty. Idn't she a wuv-vely kitty?"

Elizabeth looked around. She saw nothing, but she could hear voices outside in the hall.

"Charlotte, dear, take the kitty and come with me," she whispered. Grabbing her by the hand, Elizabeth moved to the base of the book-ladder leaning against the north wall.

"Up you go!" she whispered in what she hoped was an encouraging tone. "Be quiet like a bunny and quick like a mouse."

Charlotte climbed the ladder, with Elizabeth right behind her. At the top, she pointed to a gap on the top shelf. "See if you can climb up there, and then hide! Keep the kitty away from the edge." Charlotte did exactly as she was told.

"I'll come back for you in a few minutes, but don't let anyone know you're here. You're *hiding!*"

Elizabeth scurried down the ladder and moved it well away from Charlotte's cubbyhole. Holding her finger to her lips, she backed to the door, then opened it just a crack for a peek into the hallway. She came right up against Matron's formidable bulk, so close that the icicle fringe grazed her arm. Matron's imposing pile of pompadour-ed hair seemed ready to fall forward as she looked down at Elizabeth, whose heart skipped a beat, but whose face stayed composed.

"No need to look in here, M'am, I checked."

"Who said you could leave the dormitory? Why did you think I would approve?" She turned to Malice Suggs, huddled behind her. Malice's head swiveled like an overfed owl. Matron continued, "This one thinks she can break the rules. When have I ever trusted one of these ungrateful little n'er-do-wells? Impertinent sprout, I'll deal with you later! I don't coddle orphans, not for one minute, Malice. Not one girl here will ever amount to a pile of potatoes!" She turned back to Elizabeth. "Go back to your bed, Miss

Sassybritches, and I will deal with you when I find the bratling who's caused tonight's embarrassment!"

"I'm glad to see you take a firm line with the girls," said Malice Suggs. "Mr. Suggs and I believe in firm handling. At the factory, we rule with an iron fist."

Elizabeth walked straight back to the dormitory, but as she left, she heard the next remark. "We could use more girls at the factory."

At the dormitory door, Elizabeth glanced back over her shoulder and saw them walking away from the library — without Charlotte.

# CHAPTER SIX

### Escape

St. Gumbert's Orphan Asylum was once a private mansion, as was
mentioned earlier. What perhaps was not mentioned was that St. Gumbert's
was a labyrinth of secret passages and tunnels, and Elizabeth was fairly
certain she knew them all. She had special privileges, being Cook's helper,
and Cook liked having someone deliver her messages to the gardener,
afternoon tea to Matron, orders to the maid, letters to the postbox in the
front hall. Elizabeth learned to find her way around. She had found that the
loose panel in the dining room sideboard led to an underground passage to

the greenhouse out back—very handy on rainy days. Discovering a trick door in the butler's pantry gave her a safe space to keep her treasures. She had tumbled to the fact that the second-floor laundry chute had a secret side door that led down to the fourth cupboard in Matron's private bath—not nearly as handy, and possibly embarrassing. And the empty space on the top shelf of the north library bookcase opened, in back, to reveal a spiral staircase that took you right down two stories inside the biggest marble pillar in the front hall, where a sliding marble panel let you out!

Elizabeth could not let Matron find Charlotte—that much was clear—and it was up to her to do something. She had a plan, if only she could talk to Paulina…but somehow, she knew she couldn't. Her mind raced. Dorrie! Dorrie would be a quick-thinking help in time of need, if she could be found. *And* she was secretly engaged to Tony, the handsome oldest son of the gypsy family camped outside on the meadow. Elizabeth formed a plan.

She still had her clothes wadded up under her nightgown—she waited until Matron and Malice Suggs waddled away down the hall, then slipped back to the library, opened the heavy door, and changed into her uniform in the dark, while whispering to Charlotte to wait. She only needed a moment. But before she climbed the ladder, she went to a bottom shelf and extracted a large blue book with a picture of a castle on the cover.

"It won't matter," she said to herself. "With so many books, it can't matter if I take just this one. It's almost like it's mine, anyway."

She wrapped her things, Charlotte's things, and the book up in her nightgown and climbed. She stepped over into the vacant space on the top shelf where Charlotte waited.

"Charlotte, you need to follow me. We are going on an adventure, and you are never going to see Matron again," she whispered.

"Liz-bet, I'm gwad. She was mean," Charlotte whispered back. "I've still got kitty. He can go on the ad-wen-ter, too?"

Elizabeth didn't have the heart to tell her "no," and the three of them—Elizabeth and Charlotte clutching the silver kitten—tiptoed down the long, dark, spiral staircase.

On the ground floor, slits in the column served as peepholes. Elizabeth was thrilled when she saw, through one of them, Dorrie, hands on hips, standing by herself in the middle of the hall. Elizabeth slid the panel aside and stepped into the hall.

"Land-a-Goshen, Lizzie, get that child back upstairs before Her High and Mightiness gets any madder!"

"Dorrie, we can't go back to the dormitory—tonight, or *ever*. We can't. Please…can you help us?"

"Child, where do you think you're going to go? Matron will track you down and bring you back, sure as cats have kittens."

"Dorrie, *someone* has to help. We could go to the gypsies, if you'd help. Staying here is too scary for someone little, like Charlotte. You know Matron will put her in the Punishment Room!"

Dorrie shepherded the two girls to a corner out of sight of the staircase. There she stood and played with a stray ringlet of her hair.

"Miss Elizabeth, there are times, and then there are Times, if you take my meaning." (Elizabeth didn't.) "And this is a Time. What with that Suggs character here, and all. If you ask me, you're probably doing right to go.

"I can't leave. Not just because of Tony, but…my mother needs me, here in Gumbertville. But as to the gypsies…I don't know if they'll take you. Indeed I don't. Gypsies have odd ways, they don't take to strangers, and they don't do favors. But here"—she pulled a pencil from behind her ear, and an envelope from the table in the alcove—"I'll write Tony a note. You take it to him—his family is in that green caravan wagon with the orange vine painted all around—and maybe they'll take you in. The two of you are the problem—they'll always take a stray cat, 'specially a silver one. So, you're all right with the kitten." Dorrie patted Charlotte's head. "And here—here's a bar of chocolate. You might get hungry before you find anyone who'll feed you." She rummaged in a pocket. "And here's the key to the back gate—after you use it, drop it in the box beside the gate. I'll get it tomorrow."

With Dorrie's note in hand, Elizabeth led Charlotte out of the orphanage through the secret passage from the butler's pantry. Once they reached the greenhouse, it was a simple matter to make sure the coast was clear, then to open the black iron gate in the back wall.

They stood in the meadow in the light of a full moon, smelling lilacs in bloom. Elizabeth felt a swirling feeling—only later was she able to give it a name: freedom.

# CHAPTER SEVEN

## *Just a Scrap of Paper*

Back in the orphans' dormitory, the pillow fight stopped as if someone had blown a whistle when Simon Suggs came in. He stood in the doorway and surveyed the room, his beady eyes lingering on the taller orphans. Then some paper on the floor caught his eye. Squinting, he bent down and picked it up. The rest of our story proceeds from this one event, for Simon Suggs now had the wrapping from Charlotte's package, with the fancy lettering and the careful return address: "Feathergill's, Granger's Green."

"What's this?" he asked the Board members' wives who followed him in.

Eleanor Ludlow, the President's wife, answered.

"I'm sure I don't know. I suppose someone dropped it."

"But what's this 'Feathergill's' place?" Simon persisted. He had a high voice that sounded like he talked while pinching his nose.

"A clothing establishment, east of here. Far enough away to be no threat to your business, I'm sure," she replied.

A second lady remarked, "I think Matron got her gown from Feathergill's. Over dinner, she told me she can't get the dressmaker in Gumbertville to do anything that suits her, but *I* think she's just gained weight."

The third wife, a lady who rarely got a word in edgewise, pleased to know something the others did not, chimed in. "*I* know all about Feathergill's. Heavens, it's been over there in Granger's Green for a hundred years. I've never actually *been* there—our dressmaker in Gumbertville follows every trend, so *we* have no need..." She plucked at her dress's pleated shoulders, unaware that this particular fashion made her resemble a football player. (Even then, football uniforms were thickly padded at the shoulders.) "I know a legend and a mystery surround the place. Their garments are free, and do not follow fashion. But rumor says they spin straw into gold."

Simon Suggs squinted his beady eyes and looked thoughtful. He jammed the folded paper into his pocket.

## CHAPTER EIGHT

### Journey with a Gypsy

Traveling by gypsy caravan was bumpier, smellier, and far less comfortable than Elizabeth had expected, but it got them away from St. Gumbert's. They were sharing a berth over one of the wheels in Tony's grandmother's cart, next to a pen occupied, inexplicably, by a goat. The grandmother had agreed to take them, but only after driving a bargain for the price of the ride: Charlotte's sash and collar. Elizabeth begged and pleaded, but the old lady made no concessions—"Either I gets them pretty things, or you gets no ride to Granger's Green. It's a solid two-day drive, and it's not like I won't have to feed you, and you young 'uns eat like a swarm of locusts, like as not. No, them pretties are no use to you in St. Gumboots, and that's where you'll stay if'n I don't take you."

Elizabeth handed over the package. She minded more than Charlotte, to whom notions without a dress to wear them on were no more interesting than a package of turnips or toothpaste. Charlotte was happy with her kitten, and that, to the gypsy, was not a problem.

The cart had rolled away from the orphanage before the sun was up next morning and made slow but steady progress east across fields and farms. "We travel the old way," muttered their driver with a pipe clenched between her teeth, "and we don't hold with new-fangled motorcars or them big trains on those long iron runners. Mebbe they're faster, but they don't let you stop and find some mushrooms or some eggs or some of that corn they leave in the corners of the fields. No, folks who go by motorcar or train car don't know half what I knows about the land between places.

"For instance," she went on, "there's Wallerton's filling station beside the tracks, coming up now." At the end of their first day of travel, the wagon approached an old stone hut built into the slope of a rise next to the railroad tracks, at a place where two roads crossed. As they approached across a field, the cottage door popped open hard enough to bounce back against the wall. The man who emerged reminded Elizabeth of a paper clip, bent over at sharp angles.

"Who goes there?" he called out, shielding his eyes against the setting sun while he waved a stick in their direction. "Oh, bother, it's *you*, Poppy, why didn't you holler?" Elizabeth gathered that the wagon driver's name was Poppy, which surprised her not a little.

"Fred, put on a fire, and we can cook some fiddlehead ferns and mushrooms I found, no thanks to my two riders here." By way of introduction, she gestured toward Charlotte and Elizabeth.

"We can fry them up with some sausages I have on hand," said Fred. Elizabeth clutched Charlotte's hand, then let go as she realized he was talking about the vegetables, not her and Charlotte.

They ate a surprisingly tasty dinner outside by a fire, sitting on stumps and some large stones, watching the sun set in the west. Poppy's cart horse grazed beside the goat in a field. Mr. Wallerton's sausages were redolent with sage and garlic, and he seemed to have a generous supply, for he offered them all a second helping. Elizabeth hesitated, then held out her plate.

"You can keep your moddrin methods," said Poppy, "but the best part of your doings are the sausages you make, that's what I say."

A putt-putt-putt sound interrupted the meal. In the dusk, Elizabeth craned her neck to see the source: a motorcycle, with a sidecar, approaching from the east. The driver's coat was, she thought, a dark blue, and looked familiar. Where had she seen him?

Elizabeth suddenly knew, for—was it an illusion?—silver wings seemed to sprout from his back.

Charlotte stood up and pointed at the departing motorcycle. "Wings!" she said. "Dat man had wings!"

Poppy and Mr. Wallerton ignored the remark.

"Who was that?" Elizabeth asked when Mr. Wallerton had resumed his seat by the fire.

"Frank Merriweather. Delivers packages around here when there's a need," was his reply. "Not regular, but comes by sometimes. And, no wings *I* can see," he added, chuckling.

"He had *wings!*" Charlotte insisted. Poppy and Mr. Wallerton chuckled, as people do when a child says something they consider cute.

Elizabeth bit her lip. Although she wasn't absolutely certain, she squeezed Charlotte's hand and whispered, "I saw wings, too."

When supper was nicely settled in everyone's tummy, and after some marshmallows had been toasted, the girls piled into their bunk, the goat and the kitten nestled beside them. Poppy sat on the carriage steps, deep in catch-up gossip with Fred. Elizabeth was falling asleep to the murmur of their voices when a name she knew jerked her awake.

"That Simon Suggs is 'sinuatin' his way into St. Gumboots orphanage. Before long, he'll have the whole place slavin' away for him, workin' their fingers into wishbones. Wishin' to get away, I'll be reckoning."

"He's a modern man, is Simon," Fred Wallerton replied. "You know, Poppy, how I like modern devices. I've got to respect a man who came from nothing and went and made something of himself. Think of him figuring out he can spin thistle fiber! And now, he even has a motorcar! How I would enjoy a motorcar, to go touring in!"

"Made something of the fortune he and that evil sister of his inherited," the old gypsy replied. "Made that gray factory that's more like a prison than anything else. You can't make me love either of the Suggses, no matter how moddrin they may be. I'm just glad to be a gypsy, glad to be able to get away when I see things going bad wrong. And that's why I took these two young chits, never mind Tony's Dorrie sayin' I'd better." She stroked Charlotte's lace collar, lying around her own neck over a faded homespun dress, several shawls, and a man's plaid wool coat. Charlotte's sash cinched the entire arrangement at the waist.

The goat gave a sleepy bleat. Poppy got up to attend to him, and Elizabeth fell into a restless doze on the straw mattress.

# CHAPTER NINE

## *Sharpe Corners*

The next day, with the afternoon sun throwing long shadows across a country road, the gypsy discharged them at the top of a hill. She pointed down the slope of a winding road with her bony finger.

"There. Town's down there, you just follow the road. Not far. I haven't any truck with town folks, so this is as far as your fare takes you. And be careful who you trust. I won't say more." The gypsy cracked a whip to turn the horse away from town.

The cart's departure left the two runaways with a clear view of their situation, a crossroads on the top of a hill. The sun would be setting soon, thought Elizabeth, and the town was nowhere in sight, assurances that it was located down the road notwithstanding. She had never felt so alone.

She turned around to see if the road they'd come in on looked any more promising. Now she could see what the cart had hidden—a tall lady standing between a pair of imposing stone pillars flanking a graveled driveway. Elizabeth's first impression was of angles—the lady seemed like a figure drawn by an artist who didn't know how to draw curves, just sharp, severe lines.

"Little girls, what is your business here?" she asked, looking down from what seemed like a great height.

"Please, we need to find the Feathergill Shop in Granger's Green," said Elizabeth.

"Why?"

"They sent us a package."

"Packages from Feathergill's are as common as rain, and like rain, they depress people who get them." The lady paused to adjust her gloves. They were gray, and unusual in that the fingers were pointed and appeared to end in tiny metal tips, making the hands that wore them resemble claws. "You really need to be careful. Feathergill's is an untidy operation. The hussies who work there make frequent and, to *my* mind, unforgivable errors. Your package, no doubt, was a mistake, I assume you come from out of town?"

Elizabeth was wary. She hesitated, then answered, "Yes."

"Speak up! Well, I must say, a package directed clear out of town is a new low, even for Feathergill's. They only serve Granger's Green, and they don't even do *that* well. They have no business outside of town." She eyed the two girls, and Elizabeth eyed the road behind and to her left, the road that the gypsy had said led to town.

40

*Could they run away?* She didn't think so. Charlotte was tired and had plumped down on a bench at the side of the road, holding the gray kitten close.

"But we *must* find out about Charlotte's package," Elizabeth insisted.

"Well, now." Their new acquaintance paused. She looked them over carefully and, for the first time, focused on their uniforms. Something in her manner changed. She appeared to be trying to smile. "Really, that's easily arranged." Her look made Elizabeth uneasy. She continued, "But it's late, and Feathergill's is closed. You'd best come with me and spend the night. You can go to Feathergill's…tomorrow." She leaned over and took hold of Charlotte by the shoulder. Her sharp glove-tips ripped the uniform fabric. Charlotte winced and cried out, but their new acquaintance seemed not to notice.

"Up, now! I am Miss Sharpe; my house is down this drive, and I have a place where you can stay. Isn't that fortunate?"

"Fortunate" was not the word that jumped to Elizabeth's mind, but she could not see a way to excuse herself and Charlotte. Besides, she thought, they were both hungry, and it was just possible they might be offered something to eat.

She followed, feeling helpless. From her position, she could see the lady's pea-green dress was cut, like her gloves, so that the hem of the jacket and sleeves ended in little metal points. The narrow skirt was topped with a bustle, and it, too, ended in sharp triangles. The entire outfit made a clinking noise with every step. Their new acquaintance stalked between the pillars, on which the words "Sharpe Corners" could be seen. The gate closed behind them with a *clang* like a heavy skillet dropped on a concrete floor.

As they made their way around the first bend in a winding drive, a stone house, tall and narrow, with a narrower tower rising on the right, came into view. The windows were capped with pointy gables, and the tower was topped with what looked like a witch's hat. Elizabeth saw movement behind a window and wondered who was watching. Another pointy dormer formed a porch over the front door where the tall lady marched them inside.

"We're very modern at Sharpe Corners. We even have a telephone, which I will use to call my sister Letitia. Wait here" — she gestured them into a formal parlor. She rang a bell that stood on the table, then picked up the telephone. After dialing she waited; meanwhile, a maid appeared in response to the bell.

"Make some snacks, Elsie. In here."

"Well, ma'm, I'll have to *make* 'em in the kitchen and then I can *bring* 'em in here."

"That's what I meant," Miss Sharpe replied, sharply.

"Will the liverwurst and pickles be alright?"

"Yes, yes, whatever." Elsie's employer waved dismissively.

Elsie disappeared, and Elizabeth had time to look around. The room had a high ceiling that flung itself upward to a peak, leaving a feeling it was trying to get away from the unfriendly array of narrow chairs and hard couches below. Windows ranged along one side of the room, shaped like triangles set on top of rectangles, very tall. Elizabeth was surprised that so many windows let in so little light, but the thorny hedges outside had been allowed to run riot, and they blocked any light trying to get in. She and Charlotte settled themselves as best they could on a prickly mohair sofa.

Miss Sharpe commenced her phone call while making a ceremony out of removing her frightening gloves. "Lettie, come over right now. No excuses. Make haste—no sense dragging your feet, especially in those tight shoes. Two strange little girls have turned up at my door. One is attractive, one…isn't, but never mind. Just come *now*."

A few minutes into the uncomfortable silence that followed, a faltering footstep heralded the arrival of Mrs. Letitia Short, known as Miss Lettie since both Mr. Short and her use of "Mrs." had disappeared long ago. She was thin, and leaned forward when she walked, so she gave the impression of trying to hear something she couldn't quite catch. A dress of a watered-down blue, three inches too short in the uneven hem and the sleeves, and a little too tight everywhere else, stretched across her bony frame.

"Lettie!"

"Hepzibah!"

The two sisters embraced by holding their arms out and standing in the space without actually touching. Elizabeth rolled the name "Hepzibah" around on her tongue. It felt like a pill.

"I just let myself in by the side door," said Lettie.

Her sister ignored this. "I believe we see before us" — she dragged her glance across Elizabeth and Charlotte — "a solution to the problem Winifred called about. It will require your help, and a strict need for secrecy."

"Your call came at a most inconvenient time, sister," Miss Lettie began, "but I have managed to get away from my sauerkraut."

Miss Sharpe chose to focus on her sister's outfit. "I see Mariah has sent you a new dress as unbecoming as the others," she said.

"My dresses wear out so quickly, I have to wear a new one when it arrives, elsewise I'd be showing ripped shoulders and elbows, Sister."

"Mariah should send better frocks!"

"She always says she has only the material I provide, and of course that is so unfair, Hepzibah. If I had enough money, I would buy my frocks elsewhere," said Miss Lettie with apparent annoyance and feeling.

"Letitia," her sister intoned, "you really need to complain. Someone must take Mariah to task. Now, let's talk about these girls."

# CHAPTER TEN

## *Mrs. Stabberback*

Just then the doorbell rang, and Elsie, breathless after a run from the kitchen, came in and presented Miss Sharpe with a small green visiting card on a silver tray.

"I told her you were busy, m'am, but she wouldn't leave."

Hepzibah viewed the card with distaste. "Barbara Stabberback. Extremely inconvenient." To her sister she said, "She'll spread some awful story if we don't have her in." She shifted her gaze to Elsie. "Take these girls to the kitchen and keep them there."

Elsie looked perplexed. Elizabeth was glad to leave Hepzibah Sharpe's pointy parlor, so she followed promptly after nudging Charlotte, who trailed behind down the hallway. She could hear Elsie talking to herself. "Well, alright, she wants girls in the kitchen. Where does she want sandwiches? What about tea? What about lunch? She wants the tea weak and the beef rare and nothing wasted. She doesn't like my cooking, and she won't hire a cook."

Sharpe Corners might have been named for the kitchen passage, with turns and angles every few feet. The kitchen was a vast improvement. Rag rugs on a flagstone floor, shiny copper pots hung from hooks over a big black stove, flowered dishes on wooden dish racks, combined to make a more pleasant atmosphere than the parlor or the hall. Elizabeth saw a spool of twine on the table, and rolled it to the kitten, who pounced.

Elsie's monologue continued. "I never know what she wants, indeed I don't. Uncle Finn warned me not to take this job. He said, 'Elsie my girl, you'll regret it, every hour of every day.' Which isn't true, 'cause I can't regret it when I'm asleep, but otherwise, he was right."

A bell rang, and Elsie jumped. "Oh, no—the tower!" She bolted from the room.

Elizabeth considered the back door, and the possibility of getting out of this odd household. But when she looked around, Charlotte was gone! Another glance provided the only clue she needed: the end of the twine, trailing back out of the kitchen and down the hall. She found both Charlotte and the kitten in a little arched nook across from the parlor door.

Which was ajar.

So, it was possible to overhear what went on.

Elizabeth listened.

The thing the reader will need to know (but Elizabeth does *not*) is that everything Hepzibah Sharpe said to Barbara Stabberback was intended to get her to go away, without being rude enough to give her anything to gossip about. And everything Barbara Stabberback would say to Hepzibah Sharpe was intended to pry out bits of information, information she could spread around Granger's Green like fertilizer for crops of hurt feelings and angry arguments. And poor Miss Letitia was torn between her intense interest in Barbara's gossip and her desire to get back to her sauerkraut. If the reader knows this much, an otherwise puzzling conversation will make sense.

"Barbara," Hepzibah was saying, "Letitia and I are busy. We'll just stand while you blow your nose, or tie your shoe, or whatever you need to do before you *leave*."

Elizabeth peeked around the door, and saw, plumped down on Hepzibah's sofa, Mrs. Stabberback. She was shaped like a stack of cushions encased in black silk. Across the contours, ropes of the same material twisted and looped and writhed and, when examined closely, resembled snakes. Above the high neck of this alarming garment Mrs. Stabberback displayed a forgettable face decorated with bright red cheeks that, we think, owed their color to her pot of rouge. Her small blue eyes looked inquiring.

46

Her voice had a wheedling tone.

"I'm just making a round of calls in the neighborhood. Did you know that Ellen Biddle lost that ruby ring her father gave her for her birthday? I'm here to tell you, the Biddles are, every one of them, careless, can't be trusted. Anyway, the ring was ugly."

Letitia looked interested and remarked, "A ruby ring is a ruby ring, ugly or not!" Hepzibah glared.

Barbara Stabberback sallied on. "And when I left the Biddle's, I saw Bob Smith on the street. Wearing the polka dot coat he got from Feathergill's. Really, even if his job *is* being a clown, that coat is *too much*. Mariah could tone down the cut, if she had more fashion sense."

Elizabeth was listening so intently she could hear Letitia Short's heartfelt sniff. Hepzibah, torn between keeping the conversation short and contradicting anything said, remarked, "I have gotten satisfactory dresses there, because I am firm with them."

Letitia murmured, "Feathergill's makes *my* dresses too short and too tight, every time."

Her sister gave her a squinty look, meant to discourage talk. Letitia subsided.

"Now that's interesting," said their visitor. "They say my words won't make a whole dress. I'm the only one, they say. So, I use what they *can* make" — she indicated her snake-like frock — "and have my own devices for the back."

She changed subjects. "But, that's neither here nor there. I saw you with two little girls, and thought I'd pay a friendly call, just in time for a neighborly cup of tea, and find out all about them."

"We can't offer you tea, Barbara. Elsie is busy," said Hepzibah Sharpe. She tapped her fingers on a tabletop.

"Oh, don't trouble Elsie," said their visitor. The smile on her face was undisturbed. "She's always slaving away. Although, I am quite parched. Maybe I'll just get myself a glass of water from the kitchen..."

"No, no!" said Hepzibah, sharply. She sighed and rang the bell. When Elsie did not appear, the difficult conversation resumed.

"We have two visiting children," Hepzibah Sharpe conceded. "Distant relatives."

"Well, you don't have local relations," said Mrs. Stabberback. "And really, Hepzibah, I thought you didn't *like* children."

Hepzibah disliked being called by her first name almost as much as she disliked children but said nothing.

Mrs. Stabberback, undaunted, launched a surprise attack. "And, imagine my shock...they were wearing *prison uniforms.*"

Elizabeth, out in the hall, gasped. Luckily, no one heard.

"Of course, I'm puzzled. Surely Feathergill's could provide suitable dresses for the poor little things."

"Feathergill's! Can we *please* change the subject!" Hepzibah exclaimed.

"My goodness, I thought you found them very satisfactory." Mrs. Stabberback smiled with the air of someone who had scored a point. She didn't often find a worthy adversary, and she considered Hepzibah Sharpe's anger proof she had touched a nerve. She went on. "The uniforms were most unattractive, I must say."

"There's no 'must' about what you said," Hepzibah retorted. But rudeness, on Barbara, worked like water on drooping daffodils. She responded perkily.

"To get a cheap uniform, you have to sacrifice style. Of course, you'll get them something...nicer."

"Matching dresses are common in the Short family, just as short visits are a tradition in the Sharpe family," said Hepzibah Sharpe.

Mrs. Stabberback did not pick up the hint. "Children at Sharpe Corners! What a stir it will make in town! Of course, I'll spread the news, no need to thank me."

"Don't trouble yourself, Barbara. Their stay here will be brief."

"Oh, then you'll be sending them back where they got those uniforms," said Mrs. Stabberback, standing. "I hope their visit isn't too inconvenient, Hepzibah. Letitia, that dress needs a petticoat and some cuffs. Next time I see my seamstress, I'll ask if she's taking new clients. Never mind about the tea—I'll show myself out."

Elsie returned to the parlor through another door, breathless.

"I require you to answer my bell right away."

"I was in the tower, ma'm, answerin' the other bell. She wanted song sheets. She didn't want lunch, because she's singing again."

"Then let her go hungry, and sing for her supper," said that unsympathetic lady. "Now bring those girls back."

Of course, Elsie found them in the back hall when she stepped out of the parlor, Charlotte curled up asleep with her head in Elizabeth's lap. Elsie made a face to show they should be silent, waited, then ushered them back into the parlor.

The two sisters had been talking in whispers. Miss Sharpe turned, and spoke to Charlotte and Elizabeth.

"Girls, you'll stay with my sister, over in the hollow at Scrapebottom Cottage. She's been looking for household help"—Miss Hepzibah looked meaningfully at Elizabeth—"and she has always wanted a daughter"—her gaze shifted to Charlotte. "So, you'll have a new home, and there will be no questions about errant packages cropping up from second-rate establishments unable to keep their customers straight."

49

Elizabeth pressed her lips together tightly. A picture of Paulina flashed in her mind, and of her last words, "...*take care of the new girl. Look after her. You're the only one who can.*"

Miss Sharpe continued, "My sister will take you two fortunate girls with her."

"I have a garret for you," Miss Lettie told Elizabeth. "You can help me clear out the spiders, and the occasional bat. And you, dear..." she looked at Charlotte, "can have a cot right at the foot of my bed in my room. Won't that be nice?"

Charlotte rubbed her eyes, looked doubtful, and clutched her kitten.

Elizabeth had an active mind and an agile imagination. A vision of the sort of household Lettie Short would keep assembled itself, unbidden, in her mind's eye. Sandwiches made from sardine paste on day-old bread, served on chipped plates set out on a stained tablecloth that failed to cover a dented table jammed into a dark dining room in a tilted cottage in which Miss Lettie's constant complaints were as steady as the drip of rain from a leaky roof—Elizabeth could see it clearly. And she could hear Mrs. Stabberback's voice "...you'll be sending them back where they came from..." repeating in her heart.

For the second time in the course of this adventure, she made up her mind. *Whatever I need to do*, she thought, *I did NOT get Charlotte out of St. Gumbert's to lead her into disaster, or slavery, or awful food.*

Her years in the orphanage had taught her to compose her face no matter what she was thinking. At Miss Lettie's timid, "Come along now, girls, and I'm sure we'll find a way to make ends meet," she stood up and took Charlotte by the hand.

"My house is close by. We'll visit dear Hepzibah regularly," Miss Lettie continued, "seeing she is so much better provided for than I am. But one mustn't complain..." Her sentence trailed off like the limp hem of her dress.

Elizabeth and Charlotte followed, but Elizabeth's mind was working at top speed. Miss Lettie struggled to open the heavy gate, and the little procession stepped through and turned right, away from the road to town. Miss Lettie talked as she led the way.

"We'll just leave your kitty beside the highway. I can't be expected to provide for you *and* an animal. I'm sure he'll be fine."

Her voice was faint, and Charlotte, who had dropped Elizabeth's hand in order to better hold the kitten, trailed behind and did not hear her over the crunch and rumble of an approaching horse-drawn wagon. Elizabeth, thinking fierce thoughts, took a step back and grasped Charlotte's free hand just as Miss Lettie took a right turn and almost disappeared down some steep stone steps. From up on the road, Elizabeth caught a quick glance of a dilapidated cottage in a depressed hollow at the bottom of the steps. Shutters, chimneys, and doors were all at different angles, none of them straight, and the sight confirmed her resolve to escape.

Miss Lettie was halfway down the steps before she noticed Elizabeth and Charlotte were not behind and, indeed, were nowhere to be seen.

# CHAPTER ELEVEN

*Shelter*

A white horse-drawn wagon had rumbled past, headed toward town, a wagon with an inviting platform jutting out behind. When Miss Lettie turned down the stairs, Elizabeth gave Charlotte's hand a tug and they ran. Boosting Charlotte onto the platform, Elizabeth tossed their bundle of belongings up and then jumped up herself. From there, it was quick work to open the back door and slip inside. Peering cautiously out the rear window, Elizabeth could see Letitia Short poking the roadside bushes with her walking stick and squawking, "Girls! Come out right now! This is a most unfeeling trick to play, and not amusing!"

The wagon was dark and cool and smelled of clover and cows. Racks of empty bottles rattled from the sides, and the floor was strewn with fresh hay. Charlotte's kitten was delighted, and busily licked up a small puddle of spilled milk.

The milk wagon (for that is what they were riding in) rolled down the hill into Granger's Green. The way wound through tree-lined, shady streets, bright with fresh greens and lined with flowers. They saw house after tidy house popping into view through the wagon's back window, where Elizabeth's nose was firmly pressed.

They made several turns, then stopped abruptly. When the driver said "whoa," Elizabeth was ready. She opened the back door and got Charlotte and their bundle down and out before the driver had a chance to ease himself from his perch. The two girls ducked unseen behind a large tree. The driver left a bottle on a doorstep, then hopped back on the wagon and drove away.

Elizabeth and Charlotte looked around. Large trees reached across the brick-paved street as if they were holding hands. Under them, sun-dappled lawns ran up to kiss each house, and every house had its own personality. Behind them, a red brick with a roof like an overturned teacup looked like the sort of cheerful uncle Elizabeth had always wanted. To their right, an upright white clapboard place was belted with rows of windows, saved from severity by a flowering vine that reached off the trellis at every opportunity.

Turning to their left, Elizabeth and Charlotte found themselves in front of a yellow cottage with a wide front door and windows made of small rectangles like stacked sugar cubes. The upstairs windows were set under dormers like little nightcaps. This house had, instead of grass in the front yard, a sea of flowers, buttercups, tulips, some early pink roses. Borders of violets lined the walks, and the air smelled of apple blossoms.

Charlotte said, "Liz-bet, I'm vewwy sweepy."

Elizabeth had managed to slip a couple of apples from a crystal bowl at Miss Sharpe's into her pockets. They would have to do for supper. She saw a well-pump in the side yard, with a metal cup hanging from a hook, and pumped some water to give them both a drink. Scanning in the fading light, Elizabeth wondered where on earth they could spend the night?

Looking up as if to find an answer in the heavens, she saw a treehouse, appearing like an answer to prayer in the apple tree they stood under. Low, closely spaced limbs curved and wound around; easy enough to climb, even for Charlotte, plus some boards were nailed to the trunk to act as steps. Once up in the branches, the tree house turned out to be an endearing two-level, with floors made of old boards, and more boards nailed to the trunk to serve as shelves to hold—wonderful sight!—some old quilts and battered plates and cups. There was even a wax-paper packet of crackers.

Three steps farther up, another platform provided just enough room for two girls to lie down. Elizabeth had already grabbed the blankets.

They were snug and, for the moment, secure. Elizabeth pulled the blue book with the castle cover out of their bundle and began the story she loved best while they ate their apples and crackers, modifying its first sentence slightly to meet the current situation. "Once upon a time, there were *two* lost princesses who needed to find their way home..." But before the princesses could get a single sentence further, Charlotte was asleep.

# CHAPTER TWELVE

## *The Greenes*

Elizabeth sat bolt upright and rubbed her eyes. Everywhere she looked, she saw blossoms in a room with no walls. Where was she? Then she remembered the tree house, and Charlotte, who was nowhere to be seen. Before Elizabeth had time to worry, a blonde head popped over the edge of the platform.

"Liz-bet, I made a *fwend.* Come see."

Elizabeth felt her heart contract. She stood up and bumped her head on a branch. She was in a no mood to meet another stranger. Judging by their experience so far, Granger's Green was not a good place to meet trustworthy people.

At the foot of the tree stood a plump lady in a bright flowered dress, wiping her hands on an apron.

"I see, I see. You found Marcus and Ben's tree house! But there can't have been much food up there—I'm guessing you girls might need some breakfast, might you not?" And their cheerful new friend winked at Elizabeth, who was still suspicious. "Come inside—I'll get you warm water for hand-washing, and we'll rustle up something to eat. How does bacon and pancakes with maple syrup sound?"

Truth be told, it sounded heavenly, even to cautious Elizabeth.

"I'm Mrs. Greene," said their new acquaintance as she mixed pancake batter in a striped bowl. She did this with some authority—Elizabeth found herself hoping the pancakes would be excellent.

"Would you like blueberries in yours? I have some in the larder." Elizabeth nodded yes; Charlotte looked hesitant.

"Then we'll make some of each, and you can have them either way," said Mrs. Greene. "Let's get your kitty a saucer of milk. And after breakfast we'll talk about where you're going, and how Mr. Greene and I can help." The remark may have been well-meant, but the idea of being "helped" any more set off all Elizabeth's internal alarms.

The subject did not come up exactly as she had expected. Mr. Greene, a cheerful, ruddy man with faded green gardening trousers patched at the knees, and a shirt with a pattern of dog bones and celery stalks, joined them and told stories about bunnies in the garden, the trials of growing asparagus, the fascinating habits of snails. He got them laughing. All the while, there was a twinkle in his eye. Elizabeth began to relax, just a little bit.

But noises from outside—thumping and clattering—caught his attention. He jumped up from the table so quickly they had to steady their juice glasses.

"Did you hear that, Rosie? It's Marmalade, come home after gallivanting for two days with that cocker spaniel next door! He'll want something to eat, for certain. What a smart dog, coming home when he's hungry." Mr. Greene headed toward the cupboard, dog bowl in hand. Elizabeth looked out the back door.

Marmalade, as Elizabeth first saw him, was a large puppy, easily as big as Charlotte, with huge paws that indicated he was only getting bigger. From what she could see, he had an orange coat covering floppy ears, wagging tail, and a confident grin. He scratched at the back door, certain of his welcome in spite of his spree.

Mr. Greene had taken the time to fill the dish with scraps, and so did not get a good look, or he certainly would not have opened the door. He did not see what Elizabeth had observed, which was that Marmalade had somewhere discovered a mud puddle big enough to swim in. Leaping on Mr. Greene with unbounded joy, he knocked him backwards into the kitchen. The dish flew through the air, and its contents fell like acorns in autumn all across the kitchen floor. Marmalade, showing an admirable tendency to put family before food, pawed and licked Mr. Greene with gusto. Charlotte, Elizabeth, and Mrs. Greene fluttered about like birds, but Marmalade was not an easy dog to contain.

Until, having slurped Mr. Greene into a mild stupor, the puppy looked up and saw—or maybe just sniffed—Charlotte's kitten. It was one-sided love at first sight. The kitten had pushed himself as far as possible under the stove, where Marmalade eagerly pressed his nose. Elizabeth could only guess that the kitten struck out with a needle-like claw, for the puppy leaped backwards as if shot from a gun and ran howling around the kitchen. Fortunately, Mrs. Greene had used the time to get the leash, and managed to lasso him. Subdued, Marmalade followed his mistress to the back porch and settled down with his bowl of scraps, which Elizabeth had reassembled.

Mr. Greene, sitting up by now, took the towel Mrs. Greene handed him. He was covered with mud and dog slobber, and smelled (like the mud smelled) of dead fish. His trousers had a long tear on one leg, and were streaked, not only with mud, but with some sort of tar that had also been part of Marmalade's adventure.

"That dog has the instincts of a great explorer," said Mr. Greene.

Mrs. Greene was mopping the floor and looking at her husband.

"Henry, honey, I can't make those gardening pants last another day. That did them in. I'll just go down to Feathergill's and pick up the pair Mariah has ready for you."

"My last gardening trousers, Rosie, and I must plant those tomatoes! I hate to say goodbye to these"—he looked at his ruined pants—"but you're right."

"Feathergill's?" asked Elizabeth. "But that's where Charlotte and I are going. She got a package."

"A package from Feathergill's is something special. And the package came to you at St. Gumbert's?" Mr. Greene asked, still mopping his face.

Elizabeth felt the room spin around her. She gripped the chairback till her knuckles turned white and said, "How...how did you know we're from St. Gumbert's?"

"Your uniforms, dearie. I knew the minute I saw you. And you don't need to worry that we would send you back. No one who gets out of St. Gumbert's should have to return. I don't know what can be done, but here in Granger's Green, we'll think of something."

# CHAPTER THIRTEEN

*Feathergill's*

Mrs. Greene's pony cart turned the corner onto Market Street, giving Charlotte and Elizabeth their first view of downtown Granger's Green. They saw two and three-story brick buildings lining the street, fronted with large display windows that winked at Elizabeth in the morning sun. Fanciful statues stood at one or two of the intersections, and more peeked from above some store rooflines. And the stores! Elizabeth had never seen such enticing establishments. A candy store tempted shoppers with arrays of chocolate boxes set out on cascades of pink paper lace. Fresh spring berries and greens beckoned the passerby from painted bins set out on the sidewalk in front of the greengrocer's. Across the street, the hardware store had set out a businesslike lineup of garden tools and a shiny red wheelbarrow full of colorful seed packets. Mrs. Greene paused the wagon, then drove on. The smell of something savory—bacon?—wafted from the door of Pinkney's Restaurant a little farther down Market Street.

Elizabeth's heart beat faster at her first view of Feathergill's Emporium, on the corner of Market and Parade streets. A story taller than its neighbors and festooned with marble trim that looked like bunches of ribbons around the windows, Feathergill's was angled onto the corner, a round tower rising two stories higher.

"You can see all of downtown from there. When Mrs. Feathergill ran the shop, she took me up. I was just a girl, but I remember like I remember last year's tulips. I loved the view. There's the sweetest little room in the tower, like a fairy tale."

The cart had pulled up in front. Mrs. Greene clambered out and helped the girls down. When they entered Feathergill's, a bell on a curlicue spring above the door tinkled the news of their arrival.

Afterwards, Elizabeth sorted out her impressions. She remembered the morning light filtering through the window, making dust particles in the air glitter like gold. She remembered the smell of beeswax and lavender, and the whirr that turned out to be sewing machines at work. She remembered a rack of spools of thread, colorful as an artist's palette. Three young women wrapped in crisp white aprons moved about the room like the wooden figures that rotated around in a cuckoo clock. Every movement seemed choreographed, graceful, discrete.

But most of all, she was to remember Mariah, standing behind the counter.

"Rose, how are you? Good to see you. I have your things." She was tall and graceful, with brown and gold hair swept up in a twist, and kind eyes. Light from the window highlighted a willow pattern woven in the fabric of her simple dress when she turned to look behind the counter. Elizabeth, accustomed by now to the light, saw an elaborate system of shelves. Mariah gave them a slight push with a practiced hand, and the whole unit revolved, revealing still more shelving, each compartment with a neatly lettered label.

"Let's see..." said Mariah, running a finger down the labels. "Folkstone, Graham, Granger, Grant, and GREENE...here we are." She took two tidy parcels from the compartment marked "Greene" and handed them to Mrs. Greene.

"But I only expected the garden trousers!" she exclaimed.

"The material for your new spring dress was ready, so Agnes just went ahead and made it up according to your spring pattern. We know you don't like to bother with fittings."

Mrs. Greene smiled with evident delight. "I do love a new frock, and what you do with my fabric is always perfect. Always with lovely flowered prints! Thank you!" She started to undo the string, then stopped suddenly. "But wait, what has become of my manners? Mariah, these two girls have traveled a long way to come to Feathergill's. Elizabeth, Charlotte, here is Miss Mariah, and if you have any questions about the place, she is the person to ask."

Mariah looked questioning. "Charlotte, did you say?"

Elizabeth, who had gotten in the habit of answering for her small charge, patted her shoulder (right over the ripped spot in her uniform) and said, "This is Charlotte. She got a package from you, and we didn't understand how."

Mariah rubbed her ear thoughtfully. "As to how the package reached you, I don't know myself. We got that lovely fabric, and of course, our duty is to make something of it, and then Mr. Merriweather took the parcel away on his bicycle. He's our postman," she added. "And he always knows how to get people their proper mail. No one in town would dream of asking him how he manages."

"They were lovely things," said Elizabeth, wistfully.

"I remember — a collar and a sash. I didn't have much material to work with — I don't suppose Charlotte does a lot of talking yet, but what she does say makes for lovely thread."

Elizabeth wanted to ask questions, but as happens so often, the conversation changed direction.

Charlotte looked up and spoke. "I had to give them to the gypsies, or they wouldn't take us in their wagon with the goat."

Mariah laughed. "Well, nothing to worry about, dear. I've already made another collar and sash, exactly like the first ones. The material mustn't be wasted. Even though you were far away, the wind blew your words to us."

Elizabeth saw a look of astonishment that matched her own on Mrs. Greene's face, but the question that came next surprised her. "Mariah, how can this be? They only arrived yesterday, and the child scarcely talks."

"Some things here are a mystery to me, too," Mariah answered. "I just know that when I get the material, my duty is to make what I can. Charlotte's was easy—and of course, with her just beginning to talk, there isn't much in the way of fiber, but it *did* spin into some lovely stuff."

"Then…she comes from Granger's Green?" asked Rose Greene.

"I think so," said Mariah.

"Where can she belong, then? And to whom? Where is her home?"

# CHAPTER FOURTEEN

*Almost a Happy Ending*

Elizabeth was getting accustomed to feeling she would burst with questions, but once again, she didn't get to ask. The conversation stopped abruptly when an orange streak rushed past the Parade Street window.

"Marmalade!" exclaimed Mrs. Greene.

Through the glass, Elizabeth saw Mr. Greene labor behind, panting and carrying the leash. Then Mrs. Greene, Mariah, Charlotte, and Elizabeth tumbled over themselves getting out the door, the shop bell jingling and re-jingling in their wake.

Out on the street, Marmalade was having a happy romp with a brown and white beagle. When the two slowed down enough to lick and sniff each other, Mr. Greene stepped up stealthily and slipped the leash on his errant dog.

"That's Fleagle," said Mariah, "Mr. Emerson's beagle. He doesn't often get out. I'll step inside and give Elliott Emerson a call on the telephone."

Charlotte made friends with Fleagle immediately. Elizabeth hung back, holding the kitten, and watching for an opportunity to ask questions, which did not occur. Several Saturday morning shoppers, drawn by the sight of two frolicking dogs and the chance to get current on the talk of the town, crossed Market Street for a better view. A bearded man in a smock, a vigorous young lady on a bicycle, and a crowd of boys with fishing poles joined the throng. Elizabeth pulled back a little when she saw Mrs. Stabberback. They were a colorful bunch, everyone's clothing a concoction of interesting colors and shapes and, Elizabeth thought, each outfit unusual in some way.

She didn't have time to ponder the clothing question, because a handsome man with tumbled blond hair rushed to the scene, carrying a leash and asking his own questions.

"How did you get out, Fleagle? Where have you been?" He looked at Mr. Greene apologetically. "I'm sorry for the extra trouble, Henry."

"No trouble, Elliott. Marmalade, I have no doubt, caused the ruckus, and look at them—they've made friends! Our Marmalade is a great judge of character," said Mr. Greene.

Mr. Elliott Emerson knelt down to give his errant dog a friendly neck-scratch. Fleagle responded, licking his face by way of apology.

"Hey, buddy, stick with me. With just the two of us, I'd sure hate to lose you!"

Charlotte edged closer to them. "Is Fweagle your dog?" she asked.

Elizabeth observed that Mr. Emerson was dressed in an aging blue sweater and slacks that hadn't had much care in quite a while. But while his clothes bespoke inattention to the affairs of daily living, his eyes were clear and focused when he fixed them on Charlotte.

Mariah stepped forward. "Elliott—let me introduce you." She knelt down beside Fleagle, Charlotte, and Elliott Emerson.

"This is Charlotte. She's returning to Granger's Green."

"Charlotte?" repeated Mr. Emerson, with a noticeable catch in his voice. A whisper worked through the crowd. "Charlotte, where's your mama?"

"My mama *died*," whispered Charlotte. A single tear slipped down her cheek. "And Lizbet *escaped me* from the forfanage! We went on an ad-wen-ter."

Mr. Emerson looked at Charlotte intently. "That must have been hard, very hard," he said. "When did you…" he hesitated, "when did you come here?"

Rose Greene spoke up when Charlotte appeared puzzled. "They appeared, like two angels, in our treehouse this morning. Henry and I were spinning with surprise. I cooked them up some breakfast, and brought them downtown to Mariah."

Mr. Elliott looked up at Mariah. "You think she's from Granger's Green?"

"Her fabric turns up at Feathergill's" exclaimed Rose Greene. "What further proof would anyone need?" She seemed excited, although Elizabeth could not for the life of her tell why. She saw Mr. Greene's hands tighten on the leash, and the rest of the crowd bent their heads like lilies in a breeze, the better to see what happened next. Marmalade sat down at Mr. Greene's feet, and everyone held their breath.

Mariah gently reached across Fleagle and took Charlotte's hand. "I think we have something special happening," she said. "Because, Charlotte, I think your pursuit of your parcel has led you back to your true home, and…to your father. Your daddy."

Elizabeth, standing at Charlotte's side, had a clear view of her tousled blond curls, blue eyes with those amazing, curling eyelashes, now trained on Mr. Emerson. *She could be the model for the baby doll everyone wants to find under their Christmas tree,* Elizabeth thought.

Then Elliott Emerson took the astonished little girl in his arms. Elizabeth saw that his cheeks were wet with tears. "This is an answer to all my prayers." The crowd's murmur sounded like a fluttering flock of birds.

For it turned out that, indeed, Mr. Emerson was Charlotte's long-lost father. Her mother had taken her to visit her aunts when Charlotte was just a baby. Then her mother had sickened and eventually died—and Charlotte's aunts, who had never loved Charlotte's daddy, kept their niece.

They later decided they wanted to travel, that raising a child was a terrible bother, and had given Charlotte over to the care of the Matron of St. Gumbert's!

It is hard to write about wicked and hard-hearted people like Charlotte's aunts, so we are glad to return to Granger's Green, where such people are rare, and usually get their come-uppance. Besides, this is really Elizabeth's story, to which we now return.

Actually, this is likely to become a rather long story, and readers are free to quit reading now. After all, Charlotte is all set with a daddy and a dog and a kitten, and Elizabeth is, at least, out of the orphanage. Any reader who is content with a partial happy ending may stop right here. But, don't you really want to know if a complete happily-ever-after awaits Elizabeth? If so, proceed.

# Part Two

# CHAPTER FIFTEEN

## *Down a Mysterious Staircase*

Elizabeth felt like one of Cook's odd stews, back at St. Gumbert's: a mix of strange ingredients that left a girl feeling queasy. Part of her was really and truly glad that Charlotte had a home and a father. Another part of her found Granger's Green fascinating, full of magical places and perplexing people. Part of her was consumed with curiosity about Feathergill's.

And then there were other parts. Resentment was fighting its way to the top of her mind; she should have gotten more credit for Charlotte's happy ending. The fact that Mariah called her forward to thank her in front of everyone (for quite a crowd had formed in front of the store), *after* the reunion, seemed too little, too late, to this part of Elizabeth's mind. And, in a back corner of her heart, she wondered if she could trust Mariah or, for that matter, anyone in this strange town. Were they just being nice until they could send her back to St. Gumbert's?

But the biggest ingredient in the stew of Elizabeth's feelings was loneliness. She was here in Granger's Green, where Charlotte apparently belonged, but where she, just as apparently, did not. No package sat on Mariah's shelves with "Elizabeth" written in swirly writing on the tag. No one had offered her a home and a name. Elizabeth would have sat down for a good cry, but felt angry, and ashamed of herself for feeling angry, so she didn't.

She stood in Feathergill's doorway, watching Charlotte walk away down Parade Street with her father, and Fleagle, and the silver kitten.

Then she looked up and observed a bicycle wobbling down Market Street. The rider's flimsy gray dress flapped in the breeze. From her skirt, bony ankles protruded; bony elbows stuck out of the sleeves and bony hands gripped the handlebars — Letitia Short!

Elizabeth edged back farther into the doorway, but this was no use, for Feathergill's was Miss Lettie's destination. Elizabeth stepped inside — but Lettie got off her bike and poked her way toward the door. Elizabeth, in a panic, darted behind the counter and ducked down just as the bell over the door jangled.

"Mariah! Mariah! Botheration, where *is* she?" Only then did Miss Lettie observe the crowd outside, where Mariah was noticeable.

Lettie Short went back to the door and called out in her shrill voice, "Mariah, come here. I have a complaint."

Elizabeth reflected that Lettie was louder without her sister. She peeked out and saw Miss Short return with Mariah, who stepped behind the counter. Elizabeth scrunched back behind the revolving shelves. Lettie Short plopped a bundle down in front of Mariah.

"You send me thin, shoddy frocks! Too skimpy! Too short! Too tight! They go to rags in mere months!"

"Lettie, you know full well how the machinery works, and you know I only make up dresses from your own material. I would use better cloth if I *had* better cloth! May I suggest that certain changes on your part would easily result in you getting better garments?"

This remark seemed to infuriate Miss Lettie, judging by the choked squawk Elizabeth heard. Waving the bundle — one of her sub-standard dresses — she stepped around the counter. This would have given her a full view of Elizabeth, who edged away. She felt something rub the small of her back. A doorknob!

She turned the knob and was thankful the door opened silently. Slipping through, she found herself on the landing of a dark, steep staircase. Lettie Short's squawks faded as Elizabeth stepped down, hugging the wall. The stairs descended, six at a time, before turning sharply and descending

71

again, and again, and again. She followed them down. At the bottom, she entered a cavernous room with dim light filtering through windows set high in the walls, smelling of something like sawdust. She sneezed and looked back up the stairs to make sure no one had heard.

Her eyes adjusted to the change in light before her mind could take in what she saw. She seemed to be inside a giant sewing basket. All across the big room huge wooden spools wrapped in colorful cords lay on their sides in tidy rows. From each spool the cord went up and wove itself into flat, square frames on the ceiling. A calm hum came from big fans on the wall, and whirrs and clicks could be heard all over as spools turned and wooden shuttles moved back and forth across frames in the ceiling. The cords were of many colors, and the frames were full of colored patterns and designs. The ceiling looked like a patchwork quilt; the room sounded like some new kind of music.

Elizabeth stepped forward, then, led by curiosity, farther into the remarkable place. She touched a few of the cords—some were smooth, some rough. She kept looking up, seeing different patterns being woven over her head. Was this some vast fabric making facility, she wondered? By now she was dizzy.

At the far end of the room, she found herself standing next to a spool that was fairly whirling. Its thread—or was it cord?—was peacock blue, and the spool was filling up. Elizabeth squinted to see better. Only then did she notice the floor. Made of wide, well-worn boards extending from wall to wall, there were openings for each of the oversized spools. And through each slit—roughly the size of a ruler—Elizabeth could see coarse, lumpy cord coming up onto the spool. And, she noticed, the spool only spun when something was coming through the slot in the floor. She felt exceedingly puzzled.

By now, she had traveled the length of the room and was standing in the far corner, underneath a window set high in the wall. By its light, she could see a different sort of hole in the floor—a trap door with a sturdy brass handle. Unable to resist, Elizabeth reached down and pulled.

# CHAPTER SIXTEEN

### *A Second Mysterious Staircase*

Whatever she had expected below the trap door, what she saw was not it. First, a lot of light. The trap door gave her access to a black circular staircase made of iron, which creaked under her. Halfway down, she saw a labyrinth of pipes, brightly painted or polished, laid out like a jungle gym of curves and odd angles. She could smell oil and, she thought, new-mown grass in this curious sub-basement, rather like the smell of the gardener's shed at St. Gumbert's after the gardener oiled his lawn mower.

"Who goes there, and what d'ye seek?" called a voice. Elizabeth, startled, almost ran back up the stairs, when the speaker came into view. Or at least his legs—the stairs blocked the rest of him. He seemed to be of middle age and height, with a bright red work shirt and denim overalls which were clearly useful for carrying wrenches and hammers and oilcans, for all those items were attached to him by some loop or strap or pocket. Elizabeth came down one step, and the man took one step toward the staircase. Now she saw a striped workman's cap like an engineer's worn over unruly brown-gray hair, and a face that smiled.

"Hmmmph. I was 'spectin' Mariah, seein' it's Saturday, and she usually comes down, mid-day Saturday. You're not Mariah."

"I'm Elizabeth."

"And how d'ye come to be in my basement kingdom?"

"I…was running away." Elizabeth could not for the life of her say where this surprising piece of honesty came from.

The man in the striped cap looked over his shoulder. "Don't ye' tell me—I'm guessin' it was either a Sharpe or a Short, come into the shop and causin' no end of trouble for poor Mariah." He winked at her. "B'lieve I'd have done the same as you." He pulled an apple out of a pocket and was about to take a bite, then bethought himself and offered it to Elizabeth. She shook her head.

"How did you know?" she asked.

"I reads the machinery down here like a book, young Miss Elizabeth. I've been doin' it for nigh on forty years, and not much goes on in the normal way of things at the Emporium, or in Granger's Green, without me knowin' instant, for everything in town comes through my kingdom, sooner or later. Although I must speckalate I don't know about *you*. You seem a bit out of the ord'nary."

Elizabeth ignored this. "How do you read a machine?" she asked.

He took a large bite of the apple and was about to answer when a boy ran up, waving a paint brush, and yelling, "Peabody, Peabody, the main intake's blocked!"

Elizabeth's new acquaintance turned on his heel and hastened off in the direction the boy had come from, clinking with every step. The boy followed, and Elizabeth, spurred by curiosity, picked her way after them, through the maze of colorful pipes, stepping over some, ducking so as not to hit her head on others. She came up behind Peabody in front of a wide silver pipe sticking out of a wall, looking like the spout on an outsize teapot. Every few seconds a spurt of what looked like white floating dandelion seeds spurted out.

Peabody wasted no time in grabbing a broom from a mount on the wall and hopping up into the metal bin under the pipe. Shoving the broom into the clogged pipe, he gave a few vigorous thrusts, and a cloud of what looked to Elizabeth like dust and debris mixed with feathers poured out of the cleared line. Peabody emerged looking like he'd lost a pillow fight.

He wiped his hands and face with a spotted handkerchief pulled from one of many pockets and climbed down. "Well," he said, "we dodged a disastrification there, Bill, sure as sunrise." Looking up, he saw Elizabeth.

"You made your way back. Guess you might be wondering what happened. As I think on it, it was my fault. I got notice that Perfessor Longley was giving one of his lectures about an hour ago—and I know perfickly well that one of his talks jams the lines, especially if Lettie Short has been talkin' up a storm in the same morning. I should have kept my eye on things." He hung his head, but Elizabeth caught a gleam in his eye and an upward curve to his lower lip and got the impression Peabody enjoyed being a hero.

"As long as you've come this far, how'd you like to see how things work? Step up and I'll give you the tour of the Subterranean Domain and Domicile of Phineas Peabody, Esquire. A mechanical kingdom," he added, by way of explanation. Elizabeth looked around—the place was very bright for a room two levels below the street and without windows, but when she looked up, she saw lamps shaped like cones hanging from the ceiling on long chains. They were fitted with very bright bulbs and cast some interesting shadows.

"We were the first place to be fitted out electrical in the whole town," Peabody announced with pride. "Before that, we had to make do with our mechanical workings, and some organical." Elizabeth, although she was getting used to Peabody's habits of speech, made no attempt to untangle this one.

Pipes ran all over from floor to ceiling, some horizontal, some vertical, some at an angle. She could hear sounds like gurgling, then like rushing water, and then something that sounded suspiciously like a burp. The pipework was painted in a wild variety of colors except where it was brightly polished brass or nickel or gold or silver. Not a speck of dust anywhere, aside from the fluff that still clung to Peabody.

"Why all the colors?" Elizabeth asked.

"Bill takes care of that—this boy's a real whiz with a paint bucket and a brush, and he makes sure everybody gets their own color. Makes it easier to fix, if something goes wrong. Can't have that," was Peabody's cryptic response.

Bill was quick to explain, "It's all color-coded, with a chart to keep us clear on who gets what. Everybody in town has their own color, and the colors go by families. The Sharpe sisters always get puce, in different shades. Professor Longley gets a peacock blue, the Greenes get, well, leaf green — that one came easy."

Elizabeth inched forward until her tummy touched the edge of the silver bin. Now she could see freely flowing stuff — something like bright lint, or feathers, but in many different colors and with other things like seeds or leaves — gushing out of the big silver pipe. A drain near the bottom let the fluff spurt into a large vat of soapy water where it was sloshed around fiercely. That, in turn, emptied into a huge round drum with holes around the base.

"That's our sortin' bin," Mr. Peabody explained in the same tone that Cook used to describe a pie she was proud of.

"But WHAT does it sort? What is all the fluff?" Elizabeth asked in some frustration.

"Why, all the words!" Peabody replied, in the tone someone would use on a backward student. "The words come in from outside, drawn in by our unique and remarkable word-attracting devices, then get washed and sorted and that's how we gets the thread and then the cloth and then the outfits what Mariah fashions upstairs. But most upstairs folks never come down to see the heart of the estabblement, which, like I said, is my kingdom."

Elizabeth, dumbfounded, could only ask, "Words?"

Peabody and Bill stared at her.

"Miss Elizabeth, I could tell you were new in town. I thought you were visitin', mebbe an aunt or uncle, so I just figgered you knew. What you see here is the base of operations for the truly revolutionary, visionary, magical, and amazin' Feathergill's Clothing Works and Outfit Emporium of Granger's Green!" Peabody stroked his chin and gave Elizabeth a considering look. "I mean, you must be new to town, for Mariah would never, not never, let you out of her shop wearing that gray sack you've got. I figger you're runnin' away from more than Letitia Short."

Elizabeth felt like someone had handed her a snake, and her imagination instantly provided a picture of Peabody sending her back to St. Gumbert's. She turned and ran.

# CHAPTER SEVENTEEN

*Peabody's Basement Kingdom*

She couldn't get far, down in Peabody's basement kingdom. There was no open space. It was more like trying to navigate a racecourse with hurdles, except the hurdles might be on the ground, or the ceiling, or coming at you from the left or the right. She hadn't gotten far when she ran smack up against Bill, who grabbed her shoulders to keep her from toppling over.

Elizabeth struggled and said, "Let me go!" but he held on and said, "Calm down, and I'll let go straight away." Elizabeth scanned the spot she was in, and saw that, even if Bill released her, she had no idea how to find the stairs. She stood still and he released his grip.

"You'll need help to find your way out—this place is confusing if you don't know how to get around."

"And before you go, why not have some lunch?" Peabody appeared from behind her and guided Elizabeth (who surely would have been lost without the help) through the maze to a corner where the pipes parted and formed a sort of nook with well-worn leather chairs and a solid table holding a bowl of fruit. A bookcase sat behind the chairs, and above the bookcase hung a chart that Elizabeth surmised was a diagram of the pipes that ran through the basement, all done up in bright colors. In the corner stood a beautiful wooden flat file—a stack of wide and shallow drawers with polished brass knobs and shining label plates. Mr. Peabody pointed her to one chair, Bill took another. When Elizabeth sat down, the red leather cushions enveloped her like a hug. She wanted nothing more than to believe she could relax in its embrace and the hospitality Peabody offered.

"Are you going to send me back…back where I came from?" she blurted out, and then bit her lip, horrified that speaking the words might make it possible.

Peabody produced a plate from a basket as if he'd performed a magic trick. He placed an orange in the middle, then turned around to the bookcase to grab a loaf of pumpernickel bread and a hunk of sausage in silver paper, which he unwrapped, cut into neat slices, and placed on the plate for Elizabeth, alongside two hunks of bread. She suddenly realized she was starving.

"Now, eat up, Miss Elizabeth. We all need to keep up our strength." He paused, then pulled up a crate from a corner and sat down. The oilcans and tools that hung from his overalls rattled like an untuned xylophone. He rubbed his chin some more. "As to your question — I've got no business or interest in sendin' folks out of town. My business is to make sure their words get onto their backs, so to speak, and that's the end, as far as I'm concerned. My advice, young lady, would be for you to head back to the shop and have a heart-to-heart with Mariah, see what she can do to get you clothes that don't look like they come from a jail. We think about clothes a lot, here in Granger's Green."

Just then a cat wandered into the little alcove. Not an ordinary cat — this one had a gray coat that sparkled in the lamplight, exactly the way that Grimalkin's fur sparkled, back at St. Gumbert's.

"That cat," said Elizabeth, as soon as her mouth was empty, "that cat! How do you have a cat with glittery fur?"

"They're not unlikely in Granger's Green," said Peabody.

"My dad says the breed began here," said Bill. "Not that we breed them — they just show up, maybe one glittery gray one in every couple of litters, ever since my grandfather's time. I guess you're new in Granger's Green, or you'd know, unusual things…aren't unusual here."

Elizabeth ate her lunch and pondered. There was a great deal to think about in this strange town.

Just then she heard a clattering sound, metal on metal. Peabody and Bill looked around, and both jumped up when a bearded man wearing a smock appeared out of the tangle of pipes behind them. Elizabeth recognized him from the crowd in front of Feathergill's, earlier.

"Wesley! Glad you stopped by," said Peabody. "Got your bin?"

"I put it back by the intake pipe, to save you trouble," said the man.

"Well then, you can take what's yours and call it a day," said Peabody. The man nodded and departed.

"His words...don't get used like most folks'. Wesley carves things, sculpts things, and words are his sculpy material. He's given to reading poetry out loud, down at the town liberry, generatin' the words he needs. And he comes by when he's in town, which isn't often, and collects 'em in a bin, then dumps his bin in his wheelbarrow and travels around the countryside hereabouts, sculptin' away. Wherever he goes, he speaks his poetry, and our word-attracting system...well, acts as a magnet for the words that belong in Granger's Green."

Seeing he had Elizabeth's attention, Peabody launched into further explanation. "Now, at Feathergill's, our materials are the same as all over the world: words. People don't realize their words hang in the air after they're spoken. Wherever you go, no matter where, when you see dust on a country lane or the stuff that collects in city gutters, you're looking at folks' spoken words, after the speakin'. Think about all the sweepin' and dustin' you do" — Elizabeth's mind jumped to all the cleaning at St. Gumbert's — "all them things you call 'dust bunnies' from under your bed, why, they're just your words, collectin' themselves in the corners, and goin' to waste, everywhere but here, where we collects 'em and makes use of 'em!"

Elizabeth looked puzzled.

"I see you don't understand. Y'see, Miss Elizabeth, what makes Granger's Green special is that, oh, mebbe a hundred years ago, the original Mr. Feathergill figgered out a way to gather word-dust, and how you could spin it into thread, and then weave the thread into cloth. That's what we do. Over time, we made a system."

"You make clothes out of people's *words?* That *fluff* there" — she pointed to the bin—"is *words?*" Elizabeth asked, gulping.

"You've said it exackle, Miss. We make clothes—Wesley makes statues. My goodness, anybody could, but nobody outside of Granger's Green has ever figgered out how.

"Y'see, where you saw what you called 'fluff,' that was folks's words, drawn up by a secret process—we don't talk about that part—into our hoppers, and the hoppers wash 'em and separate 'em into what comes from each person who speaks 'em. Every single blessed citizen of Granger's Green has their own word-pipeline, and I watches careful to see nothin' jams up. Perfesser Longley..." Peabody sighed, "Perfesser Longley is a prob-len we deal with regular-like. Good man, but a lot of words."

"You mean each person's words can be *separated* from everybody else's?" Elizabeth asked, not to be distracted by details.

"That's right. No two people's words have exackly the same weight, you'll find, and that's how the spinnin' drum sorts 'em out, by heaviness. Why, some people's speech is light as a feather, and some people's is heavy as bricks. Wesley, fer instance—his words weigh so much they about stop the drum when they come through the chute. We made him that smock he wears years and years ago, and after that, all his words went to sculpture. Mebbe just as well—his speech is awful weighty. Everything works by centrifiggle force, and display-ment, and other highly scientific proceed-cakes."

Elizabeth's head, spinning to take in his explanation, was nonetheless enough accustomed to Mr. Peabody's speech to translate "proceed-cakes" into "procedures," "display-ment" into "displacement," and "centrifiggle" into "centrifugal," a word she remembered from a fourth-shelf science book, back at St. Gumbert's.

Peabody continued.

"We washes 'em—and townsfolks' words go into one bin, and then there's a bin for the words of people who aren't from town. Wagon drivers, for instance, makin' deliveries from the big city—their words go into a bin. We saves 'em for a while, in case they're wanted, and then after some time goes by, we makes 'em into fabric scraps.

"Then we sorts 'em. Then there are special processings and machinations, and all them words we got hold of get spun into thread. I'm guessin' you saw the room above this one?"

Elizabeth nodded.

"Then you saw all the spools. From there, the thread goes to looms, and each person's cloth is made, and Mariah takes over after that. Sews up garments out of the cloth we spin and weave. And every person's cloth resemblicates their character."

Elizabeth frowned.

Mr. Peabody explained, "Looks like."

"*Resembles*, then?"

"Sure as fish swim and birds fly, folk's words look like 'em. And, here in Granger's Green, we all wear our words."

# CHAPTER EIGHTEEN

*Feathergill's Customers*

With Peabody's help, Elizabeth found the spiral stairs up to the first basement, then the twisting staircase back to Feathergill's Emporium. Stepping into the shop felt like waking from an especially colorful dream. She stood in a pool of sunshine coming through one of the big windows and looked around.

Mariah was at the counter, busy with a lady in a dress made of fabric covered with holes. Large holes, small holes, every one of them edged with colorful stitching that probably, Elizabeth thought, kept the fabric from unraveling.

"I have some decorative flannel petticoats that I always wear underneath your dresses, Mariah, for I do believe the, er, gaps in the fabric are a trend that will catch on like wildfire."

Elizabeth had a view of Mariah's profile. She saw her eyebrows rise, ever so slightly. Then she noticed Elizabeth and beckoned to her. Elizabeth stepped forward and sat down on a wooden stool behind the counter. The customer continued.

"I'm certain the holes reveal my open-mindedness, and how free my thinking is, and so I wear them with pride. After all, you know I'm always on the lookout for the latest ideas. Have you heard the new theory — the one that says our planet is really shaped like an egg, not a ball? And that in foreign countries, spaghetti is a vegetable, and grows *on trees?*"

"No, Mrs. Lapsis, I hadn't heard either of those. But I'm pleased that you're pleased with your dresses."

"…and," continued the lady with the hole-y gown, "I also believe my punctured garments are a symbol of the round frames you see in spectacles, indicating the superior vision I bring to life." She paused. "Of course, I need a petticoat underneath them."

This lady's discussion of her own virtues might have continued for a while but just then a mid-sized, middle-aged lady dressed entirely in black sidled in the door.

She spoke sweetly to Mrs. Lapsis. "Hello, Maud."

Elizabeth recognized Barbara Stabberback's insinuating voice.

"Why, hello, Barbara."

"I just came in to see…" The newcomer broke off and directed an unwavering smile at Mariah.

Mariah sighed. "Oh, Barbara…we do indeed have another dress *front* ready." She looked back into the workroom. "Candace, do you have Mrs. Stabberback's new gown wrapped up?"

Candace answered promptly. "Not wrapped up. Mariah, I can't get the back to hold together. It splits apart from hip to shoulder, up and down the whole back of the dress. I tried stitching up the gashes, but it doesn't do any good, new ones just, well, *materialize*. Agnes tried to tell me that's what always happens, but I didn't believe her till I saw for myself."

Mariah turned to Barbara Stabberback. "Big gashes we can't mend are still appearing. You'll need to change your words if you want dresses that cover your back."

The lady in black smiled sweetly. "I've devised some work-arounds, so I always have new gowns, although I have to spend a shocking sum on special petticoats. Speaking of *new,* who's this?" She turned her watery blue eyes on Elizabeth. "My goodness, you're the other little girl I saw at Sharpe Corners! You brought that pretty blonde girl to town! How very interesting. Where did you come from, I wonder?"

Elizabeth sat up straight. She was almost ten, and disliked being called a *little girl* as much as any young lady would. "We…we just got here, ma'm."

"Well, I *know* that, but I asked you where you came from." She turned to Mariah and remarked, "Aren't children adorable? So difficult to get an answer from them."

Elizabeth looked to Mariah for help, and was rewarded.

"There's nothing you need to know about Elizabeth, Mrs. Stabberback. Really."

The lady was unfazed, and smiled even more firmly. "Elizabeth! Isn't that a pretty name. I'm sure I'll find out all about you. So interesting!" She grasped Mrs. Lapsis by the elbow, turned to leave, and Elizabeth saw her black dress with the twisting ropes of silk on the front—was fastened all across the back by an arrangement like shoelaces with jeweled tips, securing it over a plain black cotton underdress.

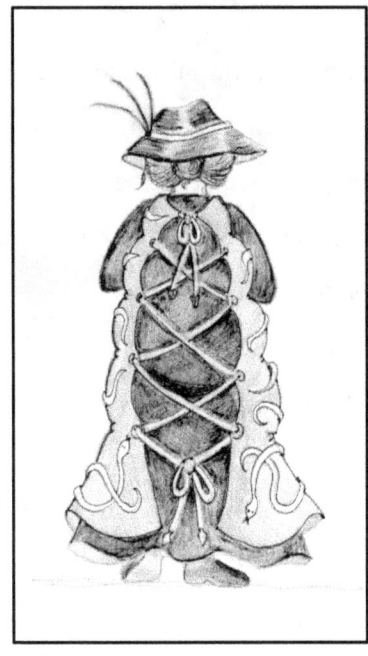

Elizabeth felt like she'd been stung. Mariah leaned over and whispered, "That's our town gossip. Never tell her anything, and don't listen to anything she tells you. Her words do harm, and won't cover her back, because, well, she's a *backstabber!*"

There was no time for further explanation. A tall man held the door for the departing ladies, then approached the counter, stepping carefully to avoid his own trailing coattails.

"Miss Mariah, I've come for alterations, again, if you can manage to accommodate me, because, again, my sleeves and pant legs have somehow gotten too long. You trim them, and hem them, and they *grow back* as if they were vines...or dandelions, or spreading ivy, or bamboo shoots. I think perhaps bamboo shoots are the best comparison, because they are tall and straight. The ivy and the dandelions are not useful analogies because they don't resemble me the way bamboo does. But I do think drawing a comparison into the discussion aids understanding, and I do like to be thorough when I explain things, so as to leave no possibility of being misunderstood, because misunderstandings cause a great deal of confusion. But then again, so do pants and jacket sleeves that drag on the ground or sop up coffee from my cup and make a mess of my lecture papers."

Halfway through this speech the gentleman turned, put one hand behind his back, and looked up as if he were talking to the ceiling. Elizabeth wondered, briefly, if one of the shop girls was up there on a ladder, but she soon realized this was just the gentleman's style. When her glance came down, she saw Mariah smiling and pulling a pair of pinking shears from a drawer under the counter.

"Dear Professor Longley, just step around to the back of the shop, and we'll trim you. Candace, take these shears and cut back the Professor's cuffs and sleeves, and then hem them right up." She handed Candace the scissors, and the Professor was guided to the workroom where his sleeves — which had grown well beyond his fingertips, and his trousers, which bunched up around his ankles alarmingly — could be pruned. As he paraded past, Elizabeth saw his coattails trailing behind him like a bride's train.

"We don't alter those," whispered Mariah, seeing the puzzled look on Elizabeth's face. "I think he rather likes them."

Just then Mariah's second helper, Beatrice, returned from a delivery. She hurried to the counter, and whispered in Mariah's ear. But Elizabeth had excellent hearing.

"Did you know that June Loveless has *a pound* of chocolates delivered *every day*, Mariah? She's sure to get fat, don't you think? Have you heard that there's a *ghost* at Sharpe Corners? And only yesterday, the new assistant at the hardware store just *didn't show up* for work, and Mr. Hammersmith is fit to be tied. Bet your buttons, that young fellow gets fired!"

Mariah cut her short. "Bea, good gracious, you know better than to listen to Barbara Stabberback! If she gets you spreading her stories, you'll have to buy your frocks out of town, like she does!"

Beatrice looked startled. "Oh, Mariah — I forgot. Those juicy stories are so *interesting!*"

Mariah might have said more, but just then a businesslike lady came in and picked up three neatly tailored blouses, no questions asked. And for the rest of the afternoon, Feathergill's enjoyed a steady stream of patrons. Elizabeth observed, perched on her stool, and looked forward to seeing what sort of clothing the magic machines of Feathergill's Fabulous Emporium would spin for *her*.

## CHAPTER NINETEEN

*A Chapter Without Problems*

Any well-written story is supposed to have things going wrong in every chapter, every scene. However, this chapter is full of things going very well for Elizabeth, or at least, that's how it looks to us. In a manner she could never quite recall, she was made to be a part of Feathergill's Emporium.

Yes, things were going very well. Mariah cleared out the top of the tower, the one she had seen from Mrs. Greene's wagon. Now Elizabeth was going to live in the pointy tower-top, directly above Mariah's room. Some old boxes were moved to the tiny loft above; the rafters were dusted. Bill came up from the basement and saw to putting white paint on the grooved panels on the walls. Mariah made a curtain for the winsome window cut into the upside-down ice cream cone shape of the roof. When all was aired and fitted out, Elizabeth could sit on her bed with a view of downtown Granger's Green, could watch the trains come and go, and see the sun set. She placed the blue book with the castle on a shelf. Mariah added some of her own books, and a potted begonia. There—doesn't it sound lovely?

Through no fault of Mariah's, attics had another meaning to Elizabeth. Remember, only days earlier, Letitia Short had promised to put her in an attic with bats and spiders. And before that, the dormitory room at St. Gumbert's was, after all, no more than a large, slope-ceilinged, attic. Even had Mariah known, there was not much she could have done, for Feathergill's had no other spare rooms. But, we've predicted a chapter free of problems, and can set this down because Elizabeth did not allow herself to notice that being put in the attic tended to make her feel that she did not belong.

We repeat, things were going well. Elizabeth noticed jobs that needed doing, people who needed help, and stepped in to be helpful. Her natural handiness blossomed when she began tending the pots of lavender in the shop window, for use in sachets. She helped with sweeping, then with running errands, then with sewing buttons on shirts and vests. Agnes took her under her wing, and had her help decide on thread colors and other interesting things. Mariah took her aside regularly to teach her something new, so she was always learning, even though the school year was over. Regular visits to Peabody's basement kingdom taught her about the mysteries of the machinery. And because of things going right, parts of her heart began to heal.

The work she did scarcely felt like work—and when she was not occupied, Elizabeth could take the pocket money Mariah gave her across

Market Street to Mr. Pinkney's for one of his excellent milkshakes. Sometimes she got two, and brought one to Bill, or Peabody, or Wesley the sculptor if he happened to be at Feathergill's.

So, we'll repeat, things were going well, at least until Hepzibah Sharpe came in for a package and stopped short when she saw Elizabeth.

"This little girl of yours," she said to Mariah, "she belongs with my sister, over at Scrapebottom Cottage! You have assistants"—her glance traveled to the work room where Agnes, Beatrice, and Candace were sewing—"and my sister Letitia needs household help."

"Elizabeth can surely speak for herself," said Mariah. "Elizabeth, would you like to go back to Miss Short's with Miss Sharpe? I love having you here, but if you'd rather be somewhere else, the choice is yours."

"'The choice is *hers?*'" Hepzibah Sharpe took offence. "*Hers?* Fiddlesticks, Mariah, she's a *child!* Hand her over right now, and I—and my sister, of course—will show her what kind of *choices* she really has. Life does not give orphans a menu from which to pick and choose. It presents them with an occasional opportunity—like a chance to live with an established family such as mine. Only a foolish flibbertigibbet would pass it up."

Elizabeth felt angry at this bossiness, but before she had to defend herself, Mariah spoke up. (She seemed as soft as warm butter when you worked alongside her, but Mariah had inner strength in a pinch.) She leaned across the counter, "Orphans, more than anyone, *need* choices. You will NOT come in here and take away Elizabeth's, or any of ours, here at Feathergill's!"

After this, all Elizabeth had to do was say, "I would like to stay here, thank you very much, Miss Sharpe."

St. Gumbert's Orphan Asylum had taught manners with great thoroughness.

Mariah took Elizabeth for a walk after this encounter. "You mustn't be afraid of Hepzibah Sharpe, for you have a place with us. Hepzibah can't help being the way she is. Zerubabble Sharpe, her father, well, he was sharp with his words, too. He started a thumb tack factory, and the whole family is just a little *pointed.*"

Mrs. Stabberback, of course, could be counted on to poke her nose into the shop. We've already remarked that things were going very well for Elizabeth, but Barbara Stabberback's interest was in whatever was going wrong. She made conversation when Elizabeth was handing her the latest dress-front the shop had concocted, an elaborate affair of vines that resembled poison ivy. The staff had had to wear gloves that week, as touching the fabric for any length of time produced a rash.

"So, they put you up in the tower?" Barbara began, as always, smiling sweetly. "How *nice.* Of course, when Agnes, Beatrice, and Candace were new, they found rooms for *them.* But I'm sure that isn't always possible. And of course, those three all needed closet space for the dresses Feathergill's made for them, right from the start, and that's not necessary for you, I hear…" The sentence trailed off, and acted like a harpoon on Elizabeth's heart.

For the problem of clothing was, oddly enough, the toughest to solve. For a tailoring and dressmaking establishment, Feathergill's had remarkably few remnants. Hardly any, really. Clients wanted theirs for use in quilts or pillows. Most owners felt fond of their fabric and treasured every scrap. On one of her first Monday mornings in town, Mariah called to Agnes, who rolled out a wooden cart full of odds and ends of fabric from the back recesses of the Emporium. Each was folded into a rectangle and tied up with string and a dated tag.

"I don't know why your own words are not coming down the hopper to Peabody," said Mariah, with her hand on her cheek. "But these are the scraps from the stranger's bin. None of them are large, but there are some useful bits," said Mariah. "Let's see…Some blue muslin, and some gingham with a flower pattern in blue. I think, Elizabeth, that this blue would look wonderful on you. And then…" she paused to consider some other fabrics. "Why don't you go through the bin and pick? If you like these blue things"—and Elizabeth did—"then I'll go ahead and piece together a dress. Later, I hope we'll have fabric made from your own words."

And so, Elizabeth came to have a wardrobe, but not the kind she saw on other people in Granger's Green. Barbara Stabberback was quick to make a remark every time she was in the shop, and looked over Elizabeth's patchwork dresses with her busy, watery, blue eyes.

"How odd that you don't have your own cloth. I wonder why. Why would you be the only one Feathergill's doesn't provide for?"

Elizabeth felt this keenly—who wouldn't?—but never said so to Mariah, not wanting to seem ungrateful. And, in the shop and on errands around town, she wore a white apron with her initial embroidered on the front, like all the girls who helped in the emporium. Still—this was a pain to her and is as close to a problem as we get in this chapter, but since she did get out of her St. Gumbert's uniform, we've decided not to call it a problem.

After a while—Elizabeth could measure the time in weeks, not days—she stopped jumping nervously when the shop bell rang. More time passed before she stopped doubting the intention behind every word spoken to her, afraid it was code for "and now we're sending you back to the orphanage." More time was needed before she stopped looking over her shoulder to see if someone—a customer, a shop girl, Mariah—might be watching to catch her in a mistake that they would blame her for at the end of the day. In a few months, most of these reactions packed their bags and moved out of Elizabeth's heart.

So, our story's main character is making excellent progress, as she should, in a chapter dedicated to things going well. The process might have taken much longer in another town or another place.

Charlotte, by the way, came to be a regular visitor, along with her silver kitten who had acquired the name Nosey. Her visits had an interesting result. When a customer came in, Charlotte would take the crayons and paper Mariah kept on hand and draw with a skill beyond her years. She liked to draw people in outfits. The drawings' details arrested Elizabeth's attention, for each showed the types of buttons, the details of seams and construction, even fabric patterns and textures.

One day Elizabeth picked up a stack of Charlotte's artwork to show Mariah, who removed half a dozen pins from her mouth and set aside the lace she was pinning to June Mooney's new frock. Miss Mooney wrote romances, and her clothes tended to be festooned with yards of lace generated whenever she was working on a new novel. Mariah needed a moment to untangle herself.

Once free, she took the papers and exclaimed, "Agnes, Beatrice, Candace, drop what you're doing and come look! I think this one is Mrs. Wanamaker, and this," she chuckled "must be Marcellus Lovelace, with lace cuffs. I see really excellent ideas on every page. Couldn't we use this as a pattern for Mrs. Wanamaker's suit? A pleated skirt would swish when she sashays down Rush Street, as she so loves to do. And look at the pattern on this blouse for Rose Greene…"

Mariah and Agnes, Beatrice and Candace huddled over the stack of drawings, then called Charlotte over to ask her questions. Elizabeth bit her lip and tried not to sulk. She almost wished she hadn't shown them to Mariah, so that there might have been just a little of the attention being lavished on Charlotte left over. Approval and attention had been in short supply at St. Gumbert's, and what Charlotte was getting would use up all the attention in the world, Elizabeth felt.

Feathergill's buzzed with excitement when another of Charlotte's drawings became the basis for Abigail Sprocklebott's summer outfit. For Abigail—a budding mathematician and an ardent cycling enthusiast—Charlotte had sketched a split skirt. Abigail was thrilled when Mariah presented her with a crisply tailored pinstriped dress, trimmed with bright red braid.

"With all the math I've been working on in school, well, that's all I've been talking about. I really wasn't sure how it would translate into a dress, but this is just perfect!"

"This outfit reflects your life right now," said Mariah. "And, wait till you see the special feature." She shook the dress out from the package with the air of unfurling a flag. "The idea came from a sketch Charlotte Emerson made. We know you're getting around on a bicycle, and look at the skirt. See—*divided*—like a pair of trousers! With drawstring cuffs, so you can cinch them up. So they won't get caught in the chain."

"What a marvel! Oh, Mariah, I am struck all of a heap!"

Elizabeth slunk down to the basement and had a long talk with Peabody's silver cat. I suppose the jealousy she was feeling is this chapter's other problem, but the chapter is over now anyway.

## CHAPTER TWENTY

### *The Havershams*

Not everyone in Granger's Green had been born there, like Mr. and Mrs. Greene, or arrived by gypsy caravan, like Charlotte and Elizabeth. Far and away the most usual way to get to Granger's Green was by train. One chugged in from the west every day at noon, bringing supplies and sometimes, visitors. Another one steamed out from the east at five in the evening. Between the two, the town was well served. Most folks did not have the money to buy a motorcar, nor, indeed, did most folks need such a new-fangled contraption.

So, when an automobile cruised up and parked in front of Feathergill's early on a crisp September morning, months after Elizabeth's arrival, it was an event. Elizabeth heard a "WO-O-O-NNK!" and ran to the shop window, through which she saw a very large vehicle, painted a brilliant leaf green with shiny brass door hinges and handles and mirror mounts, roll up in front of the store. A tall gentleman with radiantly white hair swung from the driver's seat to the running board and from there onto Market Street's brick pavement. He stepped around the car and opened the passenger door for a neat, bright little lady, busy unwinding a long pink scarf from her own white hair. Curious, Elizabeth watched as they proceeded straight into Feathergill's, where Mariah jumped up to greet them.

"Sir Wallace, Lady Lydia, you've come home! Agnes, Beatrice, Candace, come welcome the Havershams! And please meet Elizabeth—I wrote to you about her—she has become an invaluable help to us. Elizabeth, meet the Havershams."

The Havershams' arrival in Granger's Green was an event that rivaled Christmas. Work at Feathergill's came to an abrupt halt, Peabody and Bill emerged from downstairs like two slices of toast from a toaster. To continue the comparison, the news spread like warm butter on hot biscuits, and their presence changed Granger's Green like tea leaves change boiling water. Nothing was the same, and a cozy atmosphere, spiced with an expectation of pleasant surprises, enveloped the town.

Mr. Hammersmith from the hardware store hung a welcome banner across Market Street. The telephone lines jammed up with neighbors alerting other neighbors to the event. Feathergill's came alive with visitors. By that afternoon, people were carrying in fresh-baked cakes held high. Mr. and Mrs. Greene brought flowers and a tray of candied apple and pear slices from the trees in their orchard. Wesley the sculptor dropped by with a carefully crafted hood ornament for their car. Other neighbors brought homemade crullers and fresh squeezed lemonade. Mrs. Stabberback leaned in to see if she could pick up any gossip, but the talk surrounding the Havershams contained no bad news, leaving her to stomp off in some frustration.

By the evening, Mr. Pinkney had opened his restaurant and held a reception the whole town attended. Elizabeth observed that the arrival of the Havershams amounted to a royal visitation in Granger's Green.

The next morning, Mariah put the shop kettle on to boil. She did a bit of explaining as she poured spice tea into porcelain cups. "They've been away for a very long time—at least ten years!—while they traveled around the world. They left me and Peabody in charge here; they delegated their other businesses and interests to other people, in and out of town. Even the oversight of the orphanage where you and Charlotte came from."

Elizabeth froze in place. "You mean St. Gumbert's?"

"Yes, indeed. We know about St. Gumbert's." She paused. "But the whole idea of an orphanage is to place orphans with people who want them—don't look in such a panic, dear," said Mariah.

But Elizabeth was not reassured. She changed the subject.

"Where do they live?"

"They have a mansion on a hill outside of town, but then again, they have houses all over the world. The Havershams," said Mariah, her voice dropping to a whisper, "are fabulously wealthy. Why, look at their motorcar! There's not another one like it anywhere. Wesley the sculptor designed the body. Now that they're back, they'll help me with some things that have come up, and Peabody with some basement things that have been giving him trouble. They came back on purpose to help him."

As soon as the hubbub surrounding their arrival had died down— which took a while—Mariah gave the Havershams an extensive tour of Feathergill's. They inspected both basements and the main floor and commended everyone on the excellent work done in their absence.

"Mariah, adding new sewing machines was smart, and donating that typing machine was another excellent idea. I see, too, that you have chosen outstanding assistants." Sir Wallace beamed at Agnes, Beatrice, and Candace. "Bill, the pipework looks better than ever, and the colors you've added makes finding the right pipe easy as finding your own nose. Peabody, Peabody, what can I say? You keep the nether regions shipshape, and I don't know what we'd do without you. Lydia and I are especially pleased with the way you've safeguarded the Attraction Room."

Peabody turned as red as one of his apples.

The Havershams were clearly delighted in Mr. Emerson's happy reunion with Charlotte, and happy to see Charlotte outfitted in dresses from Feathergill's. (Her new lace collar and blue-green sash went well on a polished-cotton dress of bright aqua.) When Charlotte's story was told, without much mention of St. Gumbert's, Elizabeth's part was described, and she was praised highly. She didn't quite know what to do, so she looked down and fiddled with the baby ring she still wore on a chain.

Lady Lydia blinked. She seemed startled. "What do you have there, my dear?" she asked.

"It's mine…my baby ring," Elizabeth answered.

Lady Lydia examined the ring, then looked carefully at Elizabeth. She pursed her lips and didn't say a word.

After that, the Havershams seemed to take a special interest in Elizabeth, which made her nervous. They knew she'd escaped from the orphanage, so it might only be a hop, a skip, a jump back to St. Gumbert's, Elizabeth reasoned.

When things in Granger's Green had settled down a bit, Lady Lydia sat Elizabeth down for a Talk. This alarmed her very much, in spite of the lovely lemon bars and ginger tea the lady brought along. She seated Elizabeth in a cozy little upstairs alcove where the Feathergill's girls took rests. The couch was stuffed with eiderdown and covered with a marvelous soft gray corduroy that had been given to the shop by the stationmaster down at the railroad station—the product of years of trains being announced, and no one in particular to claim the words.

Lady Lydia encouraged Elizabeth to make herself comfortable, then settled into a nearby chair. She placed the cookie tray on the side table and helped herself only after giving Elizabeth first choice.

"My dear, how are you finding things here in Granger's Green? Are you happy — that's the first thing Wallace and I want to know."

The lemon bar was really good. Elizabeth's tongue retrieved a stray crumb from her lower lip before she answered, carefully, "Granger's Green is very nice. And I get to stay busy. Mariah says I'm a great help."

"So she's told me, and I don't doubt it. I've seen you in the cutting room, and the garden, and behind the counter…Here, have another bar…But what I want to know is, are you *happy*?"

Elizabeth paused. This was not a question she had considered, any more than Fleagle the dog could have said if he'd read any good books lately. The luxury of measuring happiness was not often given to orphans.

"Well, I like being busy, and I like learning. And I can be busy and learn a lot, here. I like that. And it's *safe* here, I think. I like feeling safe."

Lady Lydia, in an unusual piece of clumsiness, dropped her napkin and had to bend over to retrieve it. Elizabeth could see clearly where it had fallen, but Lady Lydia took an extra few moments to search, and when she straightened up, used the fallen cloth to wipe her eyes.

"There's dust in the air, making my eyes water. But I'm all right." After this, the conversation focused on the excellence of Elizabeth's cooking, her love of gardening, and her skill on the sewing machines — for Elizabeth had devoted herself to learning all she could. Elizabeth answered carefully, ever on the lookout for a trick question or a veiled reference to the orphanage. When Lady Lydia left, Elizabeth felt like she'd spent the afternoon defending herself in court, like a hero she'd read about in a book, who'd had to dodge trick questions with skillful answers. A wistful thought broke through the exhaustion, that most people would have enjoyed the visit. Everyone in town vied for the Havershams' attention, which she had had all afternoon, without a bit of pleasure. Lady Lydia seemed somehow safe, somehow nice. But then, Elizabeth thought, you never could tell.

# CHAPTER TWENTY-ONE

## *About a Book*

Hepzibah Sharpe and Letitia Short lived outside the town limits, didn't have much contact with townspeople, and apparently hadn't heard about the Havershams' arrival. (Barbara Stabberback had somehow failed to tell them.) When Miss Lettie minced into Feathergill's to complain about her latest dress, Lydia Haversham met her at the door and steered her away from the counter. "I'll handle this, Mariah," said Lady Lydia. She sat Miss Lettie down at the cutting table and handed her crumb cake and lemonade in a manner that demanded they be received.

"Lettie, you know perfectly well the fault is not Mariah's."

"I'm sure I wouldn't have bothered to come if I'd known you were in town, Lady Haversham."

"I'm sure you wouldn't," Lady Lydia replied, drily. "But now that you're here, let's have a talk. You're not happy with the dresses we're making for you?"

A direct question acted like a tack in a bike tire, letting all the air out of Letitia Short's opinions. She said she wouldn't go *that* far, and she *hated* to bring it up, but that perhaps, *maybe*, the frocks did seem, well, a little *skimpy*.

"Now Lettie, have you considered the part you play? What kind of fabric would we have if it weren't full of complaints, and constant talk of not having enough? We can't make that kind of material cover you!"

"I just thought if Mariah would *try* a little harder..." Letitia's voice trailed off in a whine.

Lydia Haversham dismissed this with a wave of an imperious finger and went on smoothly. "Pray exert yourself, Letitia, and spend at least fifteen minutes each day talking about things you are thankful for. Do this for a month. That should be enough for your new words to work their way through the system, and you will, I think, have dresses that will make you happier."

"I suppose I could try, although I doubt it will work," said Miss. Short.

"Lettie, repeat after me," said Lady Haversham, "I will try. I will try."

"I will try," said Letitia faintly, rising and walking out of the store with the air of someone stepping through a minefield.

The next day the Havershams went up into the tower to look for some papers in the attic, a place only reached by climbing up a pull-down ladder in the ceiling of Elizabeth's room. "Excuse us, Elizabeth — Wallace, do you really think they're up there?"

When they came back down, Lady Lydia looked around Elizabeth's room. Her head tilted, birdlike — Elizabeth was thankful she kept it tidy — and she asked if noise from the street troubled her sleep. Elizabeth answered "No, but thank you very much" and began to breathe easier. Then Lady Lydia's eyes fell on her bookshelf.

"What's this one?" she asked, pointing to the blue book with the castle on the cover. "May I see?"

Elizabeth stammered, blushed, and finally said, "That's a baby book, one I haven't read in a long time…" Then, when Lady Lydia didn't budge, Elizabeth handed over the stolen book in a stack with two others, hoping to distract her visitor.

But this sharp, white-haired lady was not to be drawn. "Look at the inscription!" she exclaimed. "Are you the Elizabeth it's written to?"

Elizabeth stared at her shoes and mumbled "yes," wondering all the while how she could be in the middle of such an obvious lie to such an important person. Lady Lydia smiled and nodded briskly, turning to the next book, and then putting the whole stack down on the bed. "Well, I'm glad." With remarkable economy of movement, she pivoted and left the room.

Elizabeth, her heart pounding, closed the door and lay down on her bed to cry. She had begun to feel like a part of Feathergill's, but now a wide gulf stretched between them and her. Unreasonably, she was angry. "Why didn't they mind their own business? Why couldn't they leave my books alone?" she asked herself. But her tears did not provide enough water to wash away the lonely unhappiness her lie had caused.

# CHAPTER TWENTY-TWO

*Wesley the Sculptor*

School started, but school in Granger's Green was as magical as the mail, and only took up the morning hours, somehow managing to teach as much in half a day as ordinary schools did in a full one. Elizabeth was ahead of her class in most subjects and was allowed to study beyond her grade level, which she enjoyed. The teacher disallowed teasing, so no one made fun of her patchwork dresses. Anyway, no two students in Granger's Green had the same clothes. Still, she held herself apart, and was glad to be free in the afternoons.

For things were different after the lie about the book. At least, they seemed different to Elizabeth, even though some things stayed the same. For instance, the shop was busy. As usual, Professor Longley had his cuffs and sleeves trimmed after a series of lectures he gave on the history of the symphony. Kind-hearted Mrs. Purler from the knitting store was pleased with her new winter dress, just like her previous winter dresses, done up in cable knit yarn, warm as toast and soft as pillows. Letitia Short had less to complain about since she had cut back on complaining — *that* was unusual.

So, business was mostly normal, but something was amiss. The looms worked slowly; customers were kept waiting. Beatrice and Candace, normally best friends, disagreed about a pattern and weren't speaking to each other. Peabody seemed distracted; Bill, never talkative, became absolutely silent, and Mariah lost her appetite and had to be reminded to eat. Elizabeth observed all this. The conclusion she drew from her observations would not surprise anyone who has ever had a guilty conscience: she felt certain these problems were her fault, that everyone at Feathergill's knew about the lie she'd told and the book she'd stolen.

She began to seize any excuse to be away from the shop. School only served her purpose in the mornings, so she devised other plans for the afternoons. She had, she told herself, good reasons to be elsewhere, and her mind was quick to supply ideas, allowing her to neatly sidestep the queasy feeling that came when she saw the Havershams. But queasy fears don't stay put; they spread. Before long, she preferred running errands to talking with Mariah. Or to Agnes, or Beatrice, or Candace. For Lady Lydia could so easily have talked to any or all of them about the book on Elizabeth's shelf, told them Elizabeth was a thief and a liar, and perhaps they all might decide no thief or liar belonged at Feathergill's Emporium.

Well of course, it sounds silly, put like that, the reader may be thinking. The reader, after all, knows Elizabeth is smart and valuable, kind and helpful, quick to learn, resourceful in a pinch. But Elizabeth had forgotten all this, and the lie she'd told colored her perceptions.

So, any given afternoon might find her in the Greene's tree house, or their pumpkin patch, which was forever in need of weeding. She was up in the tree house when Marmalade chased a black-and-silver kitten up the apple tree. The kitten turned out to be from a new litter and needed a home. Since Peabody's silver cat was getting old and lazy about chasing mice, the kitten was welcomed at Feathergill's. Elizabeth named him MacTavish. because his gray undercoat, if petted carefully, blended with his silver top fur to make him a glittering gray and black Scotch plaid. MacTavish never minded being petted.

Mr. Pinkney could always use help at the restaurant. Professor Longley gave the occasional impromptu music lesson—with detailed explanations that took generous chunks of time. Mariah was thankful for someone who could run errands, and Mrs. Purler at the knitting store liked to tell stories (she liked to call them "yarns") about the history of Granger's Green.

But keeping Wesley the sculptor company was Elizabeth's favorite way to spend an afternoon. Finding him was not always easy, for Wesley worked all over town. His statues graced intersections, doorways, and the rooflines of homes and offices. The words he used to form them became rock-solid when mixed with water—much like cement—but Wesley's word-ment was like marble, streaked with lovely veins of color. When he finished, Elizabeth would polish the sculpture to a soft sheen. She could watch him in companionable silence without needing to mention St. Gumbert's or the book she had taken.

She remembered the September day when, after several inquiries, she located Wesley repairing the welcome sign at the edge of town.

"This was one of my first projects, when I was much younger," he said, as he replaced a broken corner piece. The sign was a relief sculpture of the rooflines of the town, with GRANGER'S GREEN in elegant lettering on top.

Elizabeth, looking over his shoulder, noticed a large brick building, long and low, stretching across a hilltop. "What's that empty building?" she asked.

Wesley chuckled. "That used to be the Sharpe Tack factory. Built by the Sharpe sisters' father, old Zerubabble Sharpe. He made the first thumbtacks—you know, those little nails with the flat heads you can push in with your thumb?" Elizabeth nodded. "Well, they were all the rage, and very handy. But after a while, if you pushed one, the top cracked and a sharp point went into your finger. Then someone invented a thumbtack that worked, and Sharpe Tacks went out of business. I don't try to beautify that building."

By early October, Elizabeth could find him trundling wheelbarrows full of weighty words over to the library, where he sculpted a lion to stand in front. Elizabeth loved the lion.

In late November and early December, Wesley was busy at the train station, sculpting two stone trees to support the roof over the platform where passengers came and went. "Trees are a good symbol for Granger's Green," Wesley explained. "A place where things grow tall, and roots run deep."

Elizabeth asked what he meant.

"I grew up here, lived here until...well, until I started to travel. The town is always my home, even when I'm away.

"Granger's Green," he continued, "...is special. Folks call it *magic*, but I don't favor the word. To me, the veil between earth and heaven is thinner in Granger's Green than other places. So, folks get more ideas here than they might get someplace else. If their hearts have been hurt, they can heal, here. Things don't wear out as fast as happens elsewhere. Not to mention the miracles and amazements...Cats glitter. Mailmen have wings. Special things happen. And...words get spun into clothes."

*Except my words,* thought Elizabeth. Wesley's talk about Granger's Green made her wish she belonged there.

# CHAPTER TWENTY-THREE

*A Visitor*

Of course, anyone with an ordinary ounce of curiosity would have spent time in Peabody's basement kingdom, and Elizabeth, well-supplied with curiosity, visited daily. She pitched in with painting, repairs, and tidying—Peabody liked things tidy, and he and Bill were happy to have help. Sometimes she preferred just sitting, MacTavish on her lap, watching words flow into the pipes, or, up in the first basement, watching till she had a crick in her neck while thread got woven into fabric on the looms. MacTavish loved the basement and made himself useful catching mice.

But lately, things were different. Mysterious canvas sacks were piling up, jammed in wherever the thicket of pipes thinned. When Elizabeth asked, Peabody removed his hat. She saw worry lines across his forehead.

"They're full of words, Miss Elizabeth. We don't know whose. No i-dee. We can't get them into the word pipes, especially not the Stranger's Pipe. They bounce back like a rubber ball from a rock wall. It's getting to be a prob-len."

"But mightn't they be *my* words?" Elizabeth asked.

"They won't go into the pipe we built for you, Miss Elizabeth. More than that I can't say." She went upstairs, feeling a little lost, and never once considering that the extra words were the reason things were going wrong at Feathergill's.

But Elizabeth was not one to be slowed down by troubles. The next day she was back in the basement, visiting Bill, when she heard voices. He met her questioning glance with a frown.

"Some guy, came in asking for a tour. Said 'the fame of Feathergill's reached across the land,' said he hoped Peabody would show him how we do what we do. And Peabody's showing him! Some skinny stranger in our basement. I don't like it."

"You never mind *me* coming down," said Elizabeth, matter-of-factly.

Bill struggled with his thoughts. "I don't mind visitors, never have. I just don't like *this* one. He makes my stomach feel cold, and when he talks, my ears tingle. Wouldn't surprise me if his talk ruins the words in the stranger's bin."

Elizabeth drew closer to the voices. Through the maze of the pipes, she could just see Peabody's back, and someone's gloved hands resting on the handle of a substantial umbrella.

The owner of the hands asked, "Why all the pipes? Why bother? Why not put all the words into one pipe, spin them into one spool of yarn, and make up one big loom full of the material? You'd have no trouble, no bothersome making of special clothing for particular people, nothing to sort or separate. Think of the convenience! The efficiency!" The speaker stepped forward to make his point, and Elizabeth saw Simon Suggs.

She lingered just long enough to hear Peabody explain that, at Feathergill's, people mattered more than convenience.

# CHAPTER TWENTY-FOUR

## *After Dinner at Pinkney's*

Mariah had managed to get Beatrice and Candace reconciled, and organized a dinner for them over at Pinkney's, at the table by the front window. *The thing about Pinkney's, Elizabeth thought, is that the daily special is always exactly what you really, really want, even if you didn't know till you walked in the door.* The smell of Mr. Pinkney's crusty baked pork chops with applesauce greeted them. Elizabeth realized how hungry she was and sat down eagerly. Mr. Pinkney brought in a platter, and laughter and conversation, mixed with good food, made for a festive evening. Elizabeth forgot about Simon Suggs.

Mr. Pinkney had just brought dessert—chocolate cake—when Mariah mentioned the visitor. "He came to town in a motorcar!" she remarked between bites. "Wanting a tour. I don't know how he heard about us. Peabody didn't want to show him the basement, on account of all those extra words down there, but Mr. Smith practically begged. He asked all sorts of questions, Peabody said."

"Mr. Smith?" Elizabeth asked.

"That was his name."

Elizabeth bit her lip and was quiet. Maybe she'd been wrong to think the visitor was Simon Suggs. *After all, I've only seen him once,* she thought.

When dinner was over and everyone was full and satisfied, there was a hubbub of thanking Mr. Pinkney, paying Mr. Pinkney, gathering wraps and coats, and stepping out into Parade Street's brisk winter air. So, they didn't notice the black auto parked down the side street.

Back at Feathergill's, there was "Mr. Smith" in his orange checkered suit, talking with Peabody at the head of the basement stairs. Elizabeth ducked behind Agnes, who was wearing a bulky cape over a very full skirt.

"I've got my umbrella, so I'll just be on my way," the stranger remarked. "I was so thunderstruck by your establishment, I left it behind." He headed out the door. Peabody, letting Mariah take over behind the counter, headed back downstairs.

Elizabeth saw Suggs/Smith detained by Barbara Stabberback on the sidewalk. He twirled the umbrella in circles. *That thing is big enough to shade an elephant,* she thought. After a lengthy talk — any talk with Barbara tended to be lengthy — he detached himself and headed down the street.

Then heavy steps thundered up from the basement, and Peabody burst out.

"Stop! Thief! Grab that man and his umbrella! Mariah, call the police!" he shouted as he ran around the counter to the door.

But he was too late. A rattle and a bang announced the startup of the Suggsmobile, and a series of clatters and pops accompanied its progress down Parade Street.

Peabody, red in the face, stamped his foot in frustration. "He took our plans! The blueprints! Old Mr. Feathergill's originals, with all his inventions drawn in so beautiful — that fellow rolled 'em up and stuck 'em in his umbrella! There he goes, making off with historical docklements!"

Elizabeth stepped out from behind Agnes and joined Peabody on the sidewalk. Shivering in the night air, she reached up and grabbed a strap of his overalls.

"Peabody, *Peabody* — I need to tell you something."

"What, m'dear?" he replied absent-mindedly, still staring down the street.

"Peabody! Listen! That man's name isn't Smith. That was Simon Suggs, and he owns Suggs Utility Garments, in Albertville."

Peabody's eyes opened wide, and his mouth hung open. "That rapscallion!" he sputtered. Then he saw Elizabeth shiver and shepherded her inside. By then, Mariah had reached the police, and Peabody took over the phone call.

Back upstairs, Elizabeth couldn't sleep. Finding Simon Suggs in Granger's Green was like finding a worm in a milkshake. He'd stolen plans, and, she reasoned, he might have taken her back to the orphanage if he had seen her. She tossed back and forth till she made a scramble of the bedclothes that took getting out of the bed to straighten out. Already up, she went to her shelf and pulled out the castle book. By now wide awake, she climbed back into bed.

The book usually fell open to her favorite story, the one about the princess who escapes an evil witch and returns to her own kingdom through heroic acts and brave deeds. But tonight, it opened to the page inside the front cover, the page that Elizabeth had used as an excuse for taking the book with her when she fled the orphanage, months before.

"For Elizabeth," the inscription read, in fine penmanship across the middle of the creamy paper, "in hopes that all her dreams come true. With love, Uncle Sedgwick."

The date was August 7th, 1855.

*I wonder who Uncle Sedgwick was, who Elizabeth was, and if the other Elizabeth's dreams ever came true.*

# CHAPTER TWENTY-FIVE

*Ghosts*

The fact is, Elizabeth had no idea how important she was. It is unpopular, nowadays, for the narrator to step into the story to tell the reader things, but it seems necessary in this case because our character has no idea. We have already directed your attention away from Charlotte, because readers are easily distracted by her blonde curls and long eyelashes, back to Elizabeth, who, at this point, is still walking around Granger's Green without a clue that the story is all about her. And while we're at it, we will add that every person reading this book is in something of the same predicament. Most of us don't know the importance of our own story — and in Elizabeth's case, it is almost too late.

The following afternoon, Elizabeth returned from fetching a big box of pearl buttons (necessary for securing June Mooney's lace dresses, and needed urgently, because the romance author was generating yards of fabric as she composed a new love story), when a low rumble startled her. Looking over her shoulder, she saw Mr. Merriweather chug past on his motorcycle and stop at the back stairs that led down to the Feathergill's basement. Out of the sidecar climbed an odd character.

Elizabeth blinked and rubbed her eyes. A portly gentleman in dark spectacles walked across Parade Street. Walked? It was more of a waddle, with extra-large feet in brown wing-tip shoes turned outward like a penguin's. A bulging leather satchel bumped his left leg with every step, and, on his right side he carried an odd oblong case. His brown suit was fuzzy, but his brown hair, peeking out from under a bowler hat, slickly reflected the December sunlight as the stranger ducked down the staircase and out of sight.

Elizabeth was curious. She dodged into Feathergill's and delivered the buttons. She had the idea to visit the basement, by way of the back entrance, an entrance she had never used in all the time she'd been in Granger's Green.

The Parade Street staircase was a convenient way for Peabody and Bill to go in and out, and for those who knew them well to visit. *But that's the thing,* thought Elizabeth, *only people who know them well use it! And that odd man in the brown suit...How did he know about the back stairs?*

She had often walked past the curly iron railing that prevented passersby from falling into the stairwell. Now she turned and went down the round brick tunnel with brick stairs hugging the walls.

Round and down, Elizabeth made her way. Halfway, a landing with a door opened into the spool room. She continued to the bottom where she found two doors tucked under brick arches. Almost dizzy from the circling stairs, she wasn't sure which led to the pipe room. She tried the fancier one.

Formed of heavy coffered wood, huge hinges resembling vines creaked as she inched it open.

The space beyond was very dark and smelled like a carpentry shop. This was obviously not the pipe room. There was a sound of gurgling water. "Hello?" whispered Elizabeth, and the word echoed. She stepped in and almost fell, because inside were more stairs, going down again. Elizabeth steadied herself and took a few steps, gripping a cold handrail that felt slightly slimy. "Hello?" she said again. By the fourth step her eyes grew used to the darkness. Ghostly white forms swayed in the dark.

She screamed, turned, and ran.

# CHAPTER TWENTY-SIX

## *Dr. Brown*

Back on the landing, she ran smack into someone who grabbed her shoulders. Elizabeth choked back another scream, and a deep voice said, "There, there. No need to be frightened."

"Let me go!"

"Certainly. I was concerned you might fall. The steps can be tricky if you're not used to them."

Because the stranger was standing in the open door, with the light behind him, Elizabeth could only see a pear-shaped silhouette with sloping shoulders. Her eyes, dutifully adjusting one more time, recognized the stranger in the brown suit.

"Who are you?" she asked.

"Allow me to introduce myself. I am Exeter Brown." He reached into a pocket and, with a bit of a flourish, produced a card that read, "Dr. Exeter Brown, Underground." A second line of type proclaimed, "Nocturnal Horticulturalist."

Elizabeth was no longer frightened, but, given the situation, was understandably cautious and very puzzled.

"I saw you come in. And, what on earth is a 'Nocturnal Horticulturalist'?"

"Frank was kind enough to give me a lift. I do not do well in sunlight. Bothers my eyes and burns my skin. A nocturnal horticulturalist is someone who tends plants at night."

The situation was too abnormal for normal manners to apply. Without so much as introducing herself or inquiring about his journey, Elizabeth blurted out, "What are you doing here?"

Mr. Brown gestured toward the outside steps and sat down on the third one from the bottom, making room for Elizabeth below by sliding his enormous feet to one side. He pulled a pair of round dark spectacles from a case in another pocket, and settled them on his rather large nose.

"I came to see if I could fix things for Phineas. It remains to be seen if I can. Of course, you must be Elizabeth."

Elizabeth had no time to react, for the door to the pipe room popped open and Bill leaned out.

"Dr. Brown—Peabody says the meeting's starting, upstairs," he said. Then he glanced back over his shoulder and exclaimed, "Oh, no! I gotta go!" He popped back inside as quickly as he had popped out.

Dr. Brown stood up. "Excuse me, my dear. We'll talk more, later. You can always find me"—he indicated the door—"down there, while I'm in town. Late afternoons work best." With that, he shuffled up the brick steps. Mild rain beginning to fall did not seem to bother him. Elizabeth preferred to stay dry, so she stepped into the pipe room.

Which seemed to be in the middle of a snowstorm. Swirling flakes of white fluff, mingled with glittering silver particles and streaky strands of a profound blue muffled the whirr of machinery. A new smell was layered over the usual odor of oil and paint—a smell like the allspice in Cook's cupboard.

Through the swirl, Elizabeth saw the source of the storm: MacTavish. Perched on a wide pipe beside the big basement fan, he was swiping at one of the sacks of words with a sharp-clawed paw. The bag, stuffed full, had ripped, and the fan blew the released feather-fluff vigorously. MacTavish watched, head tilted, as words swirled around the room. Bill tried to reach the cat, then had a better thought, stepped to the doorway and pulled the chain that turned off the fan. As the blades slowed and stopped, flakes settled around the room, which, by now, resembled a factory in a snow

124

globe. Bill began sweeping, and Elizabeth grabbed a dustpan. With two of them working, cleanup was soon done, and Elizabeth spoke.

"Bill, there are *ghosts,* in the other room!"

"'Awww, come off it. 'Lizabeth, there's no ghosts at Feathergill's!" He frowned.

"There are, too! I saw them. I saw ghosts. They waved big white hands. In that place behind the other door. I'll show you!" she replied, indignant at being disbelieved.

A slow, wide smile cleared the worried frown from Bill's face.

"No, *I'll* show *you.*" And Bill went first, out of the pipe room and through the heavy door Elizabeth had opened earlier. Fighting back fear, she followed.

He grabbed a lantern from a hook on the landing, and by the flickering light, Elizabeth, peering down, saw big square wooden frames, like Henry Greene's plant beds, and rising from them, white plants like small trees, swaying in an underground breeze.

The sight was eerie, but Elizabeth told herself, quite sternly: *Whatever they are, they are NOT ghosts.* Of course, this begged her next question:

"What *are* they?"

Bill, never one to do much talking, took a deep breath to ready himself for the unaccustomed task.

"Word-plants. Plants that draw in words. Like snapdragons attract butterflies, like lavender and marigolds keep mosquitos away, well..." Bill struggled to explain. "Some plants *attract* some things, repel other things, sometimes. These underground plants attract words. Words *like* them. They grow like mushrooms, and they are..." He paused again, then had an inspiration. "They're *word MAGNETS!* The first Mr. Feathergill discovered them, a hundred years ago, and he built Feathergill's Emporium on top of what he found."

The basement-below-basements was dark, and chilly, and Elizabeth had a lot to think about. She followed Bill out of the chamber and, finding the mild drizzle had turned to rain, went indoors and up to the workroom. She wanted to know about the meeting, and so do we, but it belongs in the next chapter.

# CHAPTER TWENTY-SEVEN

## *A Meeting*

Mariah had arranged the cutting tables in a square and seated Peabody, Dr. Brown, Sir Wallace, Lady Lydia, Mariah, Wesley, and Police Chief Dogglemeyer around them. Elizabeth paused at the top of the stairs, where she could see the whole room.

Peabody was talking. A bag of the troublesome word-dust sat beside him.

"Normal, we gets a smatterin' of visitor word-dust here and there. But this" — he reached for a handful of the streaky blue powder from the sack — "looks like a big batch of one person's words, prob'ly from here in Granger's Green or thereabouts, and they're talkin' up a tornado, and I don't have an i-dee who or where they are! In all my years underground," said Peabody, "I've never seen the like. Somebody is talkin' six-to-the-dozen, but their words won't go into the system, no-how. And you know the formula." He paused. "It takes a sack of word dust to make half-a-yard of cloth, so the clutter downstairs is getting' to be a prob-len. Bill and I gathers it and bags it, and bags it, and bags it. And stacks up the bags, again and again. Then we noticed prob-lens in the plant cave. We called Dr. Brown, on account of what he knows."

Sir Wallace raised an eyebrow and turned to Dr. Brown. "Exeter, what's your opinion?"

Dr. Brown stood up. Elizabeth held her breath.

"My diagnosis is: someone in Granger's Green is in trouble. Their situation, not their words, is killing my plants. There's nothing wrong with the words, but with the person speaking. Either they're sick, or in trouble. A whole mass of word plants down below are brown and withered, and don't respond to music or other remedies. Then the words go into Peabody's bin, but not into his pipes. I'll remind you — without the plants you'll have no words, and eventually, no Feathergill's. You should have called me sooner. I'm telling you, the plants can't stand the stress!"

Lady Lydia said, "The person whose words these are doesn't know they're in danger?"

Sir Wallace chimed in, "And they're here in Granger's Green? Chief Dogglemeyer, can't you find them?"

"You aren't giving me much to work on," said the police chief, slowly. "Where do the words come from?"

"I can't tell. You know — the plants' roots draw words from all over town, and a little beyond. And some words are blown in on the wind," said Dr. Brown.

The police chief frowned. "Folks, you know, Granger's Green works because we are a town full of people who *trust* each other, and, for the most part, we *can* trust each other. Of course, there's the occasional bad apple" (he might have been thinking of Barbara Stabberback) "but the fabric of trust holds, and keeps even the bad apples from doing much harm.

"And you know, better than anybody, how much depends on Feathergill's. Everybody's life shows up in their words, and their words show up in their cloth. You folks around this table, you know more about our town than the mayor, or me, and you know before we do. My job is easy because of Feathergill's. People's problems show up in their cloth and usually get fixed before they ever show up on a 'Wanted' poster or in a jail cell.

"That being said, I'll investigate. I have some ideas. I'll look into the old Sharpe Tack factory, and I'll ask Barbara Stabberback what she knows."

"She spent some time talkin' to the fella who stole our plans," Peabody added. He looked discouraged. "Bill and I are 'runnin' out of i-dees, and space. All these sacks take *room*. We can't throw out vallable words, but

128

there's no place to put 'em! I can't make 'em go where they don't wanna go, not if I had help from hope or hailstones."

Dr. Brown stood up. "My day is just beginning. I hope to help the plants with fresh sawdust and cello music."

# CHAPTER TWENTY-EIGHT

*Dr. Brown's Cave*

The next day, Elizabeth was tired and got up late. School, in Granger's Green, didn't meet at all in December, so she knew she had a whole day in front of her to explore the mystery surrounding Feathergill's Emporium. *To whom did the extra words belong? Where were her own words? What could endanger the wonderful operation of Dr. Brown's Plant Kingdom, Peabody's Basement Kingdom, and Mariah's amazing garment-making establishment?*

She knew Dr. Brown, being "nocturnal," slept during the day. So, she spent the morning running errands for Mariah, then helped Mr. Pinkney with a batch of cupcakes. Her biggest questions, she felt sure, could be answered in the place she knew least about, so late that afternoon she headed down the outside staircase. Standing at his door, she heard the faint strains of Dr. Brown's cello music. She hesitated, then knocked.

After a while, the ancient oak door creaked open, and Dr. Brown, his eyes hidden by his odd round glasses, beckoned her in.

"I thought I might see you today," he said.

He turned and led the way down wooden stairs more like a ladder than a staircase, and when they reached the bottom, Elizabeth saw what she hadn't seen before: this wasn't a room, but a cave. She could hear the gurgle of an underground stream, and walls of solid rock rose up to form an arched ceiling of stone, ten feet overhead. Light from wall sconces revealed walls striped with veins of pink and blue. The good woodshop smell she had noticed the day before was compounded by a clean, beach-y smell, and the ground under her feet was, indeed, sandy.

The mysterious white plants towered over her head. Dr. Brown reached up and plucked one fan-shaped leaf, soft, and fuzzy. A white powder rubbed off.

"This is where Feathergill's starts. These fungus trees—they're really very special mushrooms—draw words up through their roots, roots that stretch out for miles. Old Mr. Feathergill discovered them, a century ago, and he built Feathergill's over these remarkable plants, built them frames to grow in, filled the frames with oak sawdust. It's good food for them.

"That's what you wanted to know, isn't it? Bill told me you'd asked. I can indeed see how you thought of ghosts, but I assure you, nothing scary here."

Elizabeth was quiet. "Then, what do *you* do?"

"I *propagate*. I help the plant kingdom. These plants, for instance, love cello concertos. Most plants do. And I travel, looking after rare plants all over the countryside. What you have in Granger's Green is unique."

Elizabeth exclaimed, "They're beautiful!"

"I'm glad you see that. Not everyone can, and I exert myself to keep unfriendly folks out of this room. Peabody and I keep this cave a little bit secret.

"That dust on your fingers," Dr. Brown continued, handing her a crisp, clean handkerchief with an embroidered "B" in the corner, "is the stuff Peabody spins into cloth." His voice was extraordinarily soothing. "The plants draw the words in through their roots and turn them into powder. We funnel the powder over to Phineas"—he pointed to what must have been the other end of Mr. Peabody's word chute, high overhead—"where his marvelous machinery takes over," he said.

"And Mr. Peabody's machinery separates everybody's words, gets them into the right pipes, I know," Elizabeth went on, "but what about the extra words coming in?"

Dr. Brown frowned. "I don't know, my dear, but I do know one thing. It has to do with *you*."

"Me?"

"Yes. You see, we have two problems: someone's words are jamming the system. Those words carry a deep trouble, killing my plants. Look." He pointed to a patch, in the middle of a grove of the white, waving word-plants, where collapsed plants lay flat, brown, and shriveled. Seeing her inquiring look, Dr. Brown continued. "I don't know what's the matter. But Phineas checks the plants periodically. When he saw plants dying, he called me. There's nothing wrong with the words coming through the system, but something is *very* wrong with the speaker's situation. Something toxic, something poisonous, is being pulled through my plants with those words, and it's killing them. If this continues, logically, Feathergill's will be no more. The system can't run without my plants.

"And then there's our second problem, one you know well: *your* words are nowhere to be found. We don't know why. I was hoping to ask where you come from?"

No good answer came to mind, so Elizabeth just shook her head. Then she shivered, and Dr. Brown offered her his fuzzy brown jacket. But the chill had started in her heart and would need more than a wrap. She left, and spent the afternoon in the tree house.

# CHAPTER TWENTY-NINE

*Kidnapped!*

The next day, Tuesday, Mariah mentioned a shipment of embroidery thread arriving on the noon train. Elizabeth volunteered to go, and Mariah, glancing at the clock on the wall, accepted her offer, but made a stipulation.

"Come straight back when you've got the thread; don't stop for a milkshake today. I'm going to need you here at half-past noon, but you'll have plenty of time, and I do so appreciate the help."

Elizabeth wheeled the store's delivery cart through the streets of Granger's Green, wearing her Feathergill's apron. Every person she met wore clothing from the Emporium, and every outfit reflected the personality of its wearer.

*Except mine,* thought Elizabeth. *Mine is another orphan outfit, contrived from scraps of other people's words, nothing of my own. I don't belong here, and my pipeline in the basement is empty, and no beautiful fabric shows up in the store to be made into a dress for me.* A single self-pitying tear slid down her cheek, and she wished she were as transparent as window glass. *So people would just look through me,* she thought. She bit her lip and put her energy into holding back more tears as she waited on the train station platform.

Perhaps because her thoughts were turned inward, she did not notice the passengers who got off the noon train. As she stared glumly at the baggage and cargo in front of her, a violent tug pulled her backwards. Someone yanked her across the platform by the strap on her apron, her heels leaving scuff marks all the way to an empty side platform. Strong hands spun her around, and she found herself face to face with…the Matron of St. Gumbert's Orphan Asylum!

Matron's face was the same maroon as her traveling cloak. Her breath, smelling strongly of onions, blasted Elizabeth as she hissed.

"I've got you, troublesome, meddlesome wench! You may very well think you can escape, but I assure you, that is not the case. You will return with me, back to the orphanage *where you belong.*"

Matron held Elizabeth's wrists with one hand and, with the other, whipped off the traveling cloak with the finesse of a bullfighter. It was voluminous (as was necessary for getting around all of Matron). Elizabeth was spun around until she was dizzy, and found herself wrapped up and carried off like a roll of carpet. The rough wool tasted of cheap cherry cough syrup and sardines where Matron's hand forced a fold into her mouth. The jet-black fringe felt like icicles digging into her arms and legs.

From the sound, Matron was speaking through clenched teeth. "You will find your new life at St. Gumbert's very different from the one you enjoyed before. Cook will not need your help, your presence in school will be mandatory, and we will watch you closely every minute of every day. Your cot will be in the locked basement every night. You will not escape."

Panic had swallowed Elizabeth's self-pity. She couldn't shout and couldn't kick; struggling only got her pinched tighter in the musty cloak.

In very few paces she was dropped onto a hard surface, and then she felt a rumbling beneath her that could only mean she was being conveyed somewhere in a carriage. Elizabeth settled into thinking how to get free. She was still wrapped up like a sausage roll. The odd thing was that although she was cocooned in a wool cloak, she felt *cold.* Especially where the cloak touched, which caused her to wriggle. A harsh "Stop that!" greeted every movement.

Gradually she became aware of other voices, someone for Matron to talk with in hushed murmurs, someone else who seemed to be on the receiving end of a scolding. Elizabeth caught a phrase here and there — "Impossible!" — "most inconvenient" — "She can't be left!" — "Don't dawdle!" and, "Suggs" — but could make nothing of them.

The ride came to an abrupt halt with the sound of the carriage door opening, then closing, and then, the familiar sound of the bell over the door at Feathergill's! Elizabeth struggled energetically, spurred to action by the realization that she was close to the only place that had ever been a home. To her surprise, the cape shredded easily, although her left shoe came off in her struggle. *If I can get out of this wrapping, I can get out of the carriage and run,* she thought, *even if I only have one shoe.* In very little time, she had freed her hands and was able to pull the cloak out of her mouth and away from her face.

But when she emerged from the cloak's cocoon, she found herself staring into the face of Hepzibah Sharpe.

Board of Governors' Daywear & Eveningwear

# CHAPTER THIRTY

### *Meeting with the Board*

Mariah, unaware of Elizabeth's plight outside the door, watched Matron enter Feathergill's with some dismay. We have not, in this story, spent much time in Mariah's thoughts, mostly because, well, a story should be exciting at every turn, and Mariah's thoughts were almost always peaceful. Her clothing draped like the folds on a gracious Greek statue, and her thoughts followed the same lines. But at this point in Elizabeth's story, Mariah did not feel peaceful. She was almost abrupt as she gestured Matron past the counter.

She frowned and turned to peer out the shop window for the sixth time in as many minutes.

Matron's arrival was an event to arrest everyone's attention—she had not been seen at Feathergill's in fifteen years, not since she had come in to demand a replica of the purple dress that now threatened to burst at her waist and hips. She had left that day in an angry huff after being told the shop did not produce dresses on demand. She was in no better humor at the moment. Mariah had foreseen her mood, which had not made meeting preparations any easier. Not to mention the arrival, an hour earlier, of the entire St. Gumbert's Asylum Board of Governors, last seen in this book on the evening of Elizabeth and Charlotte's daring escape. They had entered Feathergill's together and requested glasses of lemonade and all manner of refreshments brought over from Pinkney's by Agnes, Beatrice, and Candace. They were now ensconced in the back room used for cutting, fitting, and sewing, around the cutting table from which the sewing notions and fabrics had, once again, been cleared away.

All this would normally have been met with Mariah's usual calm. But added to the situation we've described — the disruption of the day's work, the addition of six cranky visitors, the arrival of a peevish and difficult lady — was the fact that Elizabeth was nowhere to be found. *I know I told her, most particularly, to be back by 12:30, and she's never late,* thought Mariah, looking up and down Market Street. *It's not like her, not like her at all.*

Her attention was called back to the situation at hand by the rasping sound of the Matron's voice.

"Well, Mariah. I've arrived, at Wallace and Lydia's request, but this meeting is most inconvenient. And an urgent situation with the orphans has arisen. I only have a very few moments to spare before I need to return to St. Gumbert's. I'll speak to the Havershams and be on my way."

"The Havershams," said Mariah, "have been called out of town by their own urgent business. But everyone else is waiting for you in the workroom."

Matron's eyes widened.

"Everyone else?"

"I only know the Havershams felt the situation was urgent, and…" Mariah could be seen to hesitate, "'mandatory' was the word they told me to use. The orphanage Board of Governors is here."

Matron paused. She pursed her lips. Her hands clutched at her bag.

"Just a moment," she said. "My sister is waiting in the carriage, and I must tell her about this delay. A most inconvenient development," she muttered. Her bustling exit set the shop bell to jangling violently. Her return, a few minutes later, had the same effect.

"I've explained to Hepzibah, but we are both annoyed. I sincerely hope this meeting will be short."

Mariah said nothing as she ushered Matron back to the cutting table, where the Board of Directors sat in an assortment of splashy outfits. The scene reminded Mariah, briefly, of wallpaper samples spread out on a table.

Had Elizabeth been present, she would have been as impressed by their day outfits as she had been, the night of her escape, by their evening dress. The three ladies of the group had persuaded their dressmakers to take shiny materials patterned in stripes and checks and sculpt those fabrics with tucks and pleats and frills till the result resembled origami paper sculptures of great complexity, all with the fashionable narrow skirts that made walking very nearly impossible. The male Board members were resplendent in big plaids and bold stripes, set off by bright silk neckties of gold, red, and purple.

The gentleman with the largest mustache and the purple necktie nearly covered by his beard, the Board president, Lemuel Ludlow — spoke.

"Well, I see we have convened…" He hesitated. "…at the Haversham's request. They left us instructions, and an agenda, which we are bound to fulfill, seeing this Board serves at their pleasure. Although I must say…" He broke off and coughed into his shirtsleeve, which was bright yellow and studded with a large gold-and-emerald cufflink.

"Perhaps *I* must say," interrupted one of the ladies. "That this whole arrangement is excessively inconvenient, and defies common sense, seeing we could easily have met at St. Gumbert's, without a two-hour train trip!"

Mariah, who had seated herself at the back of the room, spoke up. "The Havershams had definite reasons for asking you to travel to Granger's Green, and I'm here to represent them. They did ask me to apologize for their absence."

Several sniffs were heard around the room. The Board president cleared his throat. "Well, since we *are* all here, we might just as well begin." He shuffled through some papers piled in front of him and pulled one out with the air of extracting a splinter from an infected finger.

"Ah! Here. The Havershams received this a few days ago, and called us immediately." He held the letter at arm's length and read aloud:

*To the Havershams, at the House on the Hill, Granger's Green*

*There's a lot you ought to know about St. Gumbert's, and I suppose it's up to me to tell you. I don't know who else will, and folks in charge need to know about the way things stand at the orphanage, if you ask me.*

*I've worked here a year. That's a long time, compared to anybody except Cook and Matron, or so I'm told. I started as kitchen maid, then got to be housemaid, and now I'm the housekeeper.*

*We have forty-five girls at St. Gumbert's, and none of them get a decent meal in a day. Their gruel in the morning is thin except when it's lumpy. Their lunches and dinners are made of old vegetables and moldy wheat, which is all there is in our kitchen anymore. They never get a sweet or a cookie. The girls are looking thin and puny, if you ask me.*

*But there's always quail and chocolate for the Matron's dinner.*

*Our tradesmen aren't getting paid. Maybe that's why they're delivering old food, or not delivering at all. The girls have outgrown last year's uniforms, and don't have pencils for the schoolroom, or bootlaces or bonnets, and it doesn't look likely they'll be getting any, if you ask me.*

*But there's always fancy bath salts and feathered hats for Matron.*

*The orphans work at sweeping and scrubbing all the time, without getting much in the way of schooling, and no time at all for playing, which is not allowed. The schoolmistress is fit to be tied and threatens to quit every other day. She's a saint to stay on, if you ask me.*

142

*And she keeps on asking me if I know what becomes of the older girls. She seems to think they're disappearing. I don't know about that, not seeing too much of them, so don't ask me about that. But I see Simon Suggs here, about once a month. It does seem fishy, if you ask me.*

*The other maids have already quit, so it's just me left to write this letter, 'cause I can't see Cook stirring up trouble.*

*The Matron is fond of carriage rides and dining out. She shoos me out of her office when I try to tell her things can't go on like this. She would fire me in a minute if she could find anybody to take my place, but that won't be easy. I only oblige because my intended, Tony Overgarden, is the groundskeeper now, and my mom lives in Gumbertville, so I have to stay close. We try to help the girls, but we can't do enough, so I'm taking it upon myself to write to you after finding your name and where to direct the letter in the files Matron keeps hidden. If you fire me for this, I'll still think I did the best I could.*

*Sincerely,*
*Dorothy O'Rourke*
*Housekeeper at St. Gumbert's*

Matron's face had gotten redder than usual as he read. The gentleman in the gold necktie spoke.

"You can imagine our chagrin when the Havershams sent this to us. After all, you have been Matron and Headmistress for twelve years, and the Board has never found reason to complain of your management. The place was kept quiet; orphans seemed to have been placed in, er, service positions when they were of age, the budget balanced, and what complaints we heard we, er, attributed to malcontents and grumps."

He paused and cleared his throat. "But, the information in this letter is impossible to dismiss. A reliable source is telling us the orphaned girls entrusted to our care are forced to work and are not *allowed* to play, are fed unpalatable food, and are not taught anything that would allow them to be more than maids and housekeepers. And since the Havershams are not present, we, that is, the Board, are in the awkward position of having to deal with this meeting.

"Furthermore, you never found the orphan who disappeared the night of our last visit, and, in fact, you seem to lose orphans left and right!"

"You can see there are charges there that need to be answered. We can't simply ignore such statements." The gentleman in the red necktie stroked his sideburns.

"You can see we can't really blame Sir Wallace and Lady Lydia for wanting a meeting," said a lady in green stripes.

"You can see, surely, that we need some answers," said a lady in pink pleats.

"Because, according to our instructions from the Havershams, you should be relieved of your position…"

As if to underline this statement, the bell over the street door jingled faintly.

A lady in bronze-colored flounces interjected, "Let go!"

A gentleman in a bright blue suit added, "Fired!"

The Board president continued "…unless you can give us some answers."

Matron licked her lips and clutched her purse. She began to speak what turned out to be a random collection of thoughts: "Orphans are nasty little beasts, and they *like* lima beans! I have stayed within my budget! I give Gumbertville maids and housekeepers! Orphans are ungrateful! Servants are spiteful and ungrateful, and Dorrie is the worst of them all!"

# CHAPTER THIRTY-ONE

## *Elsie's Dilemma*

Back in the carriage, Elizabeth pushed aside the shredded cape and sat up. She stared in horror at Hepzibah Sharpe.

"You are gawping like a fish. Most unattractive." She paused in the act of removing a studded green belt from her narrow waist. Grabbing Elizabeth's wrist, she cinched the belt around it.

"You will need your energy and strength to adjust to being back at St. Gumbert's," Miss Sharpe began. "For that is where you belong and where you are going. Winifred was a fool not to bring you back months ago."

Elizabeth's face must have shown astonishment. In her months at Feathergill's, she had lost the habit of hiding her feelings.

"No need for surprise," Hepzibah continued. "We always knew where you were. Winifred is my sister, although the brains of the family seem to have bypassed my sisters and rested with me."

This was the moment when Matron came out of Feathergill's to tell Hepzibah about the meeting. The carriage door opened, and she poked her head inside. Hepzibah reached over, grabbed Elizabeth's wrist, then leaned the other way to heed Matron. Elizabeth leaned toward the opposite door with the thought of yelling for help, but Hepzibah's sharp fingertips cut into her skin when she moved. She resigned herself to sitting and trying to listen while behind gloved hands, the two sinister sisters held a whispered conference. Elizabeth got the idea that a plan had changed. Hepzibah Sharpe was visibly annoyed—a mood not easy to tell from her normal one.

Winifred, also known as Matron, stepped away from the carriage. The jingle of the Feathergill's bell announced her return to the shop. Elizabeth couldn't help herself. She asked Hepzibah, "You and Matron are...*sisters?*"

"Apparently hers is not the only one weak brain. Yes. We let you think you had a home at Feathergill's—and we were saved the expense of keeping you—until we made arrangements to bring you back and keep you contained, so to speak, in the orphanage."

Hepzibah Sharpe paused. She smoothed her starched skirt. A smile that could only be described as sly stretched her thin lips the tiniest bit.

"We'll keep you in your proper place until we get you back to St. Gumbert's. Because, don't you see, you really have nowhere to go. Do not entertain the idea that Feathergill's will seek you out to bring you back. They don't want you. They only took you in until we could come and get you. Their mistake was being nice to you. Orphans have no right to uppity ideas. You belong to us by a law that cannot be challenged, which Feathergill's knows. We should have taken you back immediately, but Winifred is seldom free to leave her duties."

These words cut like a sharp pair of shears. Elizabeth's situation had turned from a predicament, one that she could squeeze out of, as she had so many times back at St. Gumbert's, into a hopeless life-sentence that would never end or change. They sat in chilled silence for some little time. Hepzibah Sharpe's words, calculated to pierce, had done their job.

Then the carriage door opened a crack, and Elsie the housemaid's pudgy nose appeared in the gap.

"S'cuse me, ma'm, and I'm very extremely sorry to come back—no, I don't have the package—but I think you ought to know…"

"Know WHAT?"

"Well, I was just inside, here at the Emporium—"

"Feathergill's?"

"Yes'm, Feathergill's, and I was waiting for to pick up the package you sent me for, but there wasn't nobody…"

"Anybody…" Hepzibah Sharpe would have corrected bad grammar on her way out of a burning building. The correction went over Elsie's head.

146

"It wasn't *anybody* who wasn't there, ma'm, it was *nobody*…*Nobody* was behind that counter where they hand out the clothes, and, and, *somebody* is always there. They're ever so particular, always have been, about *somebody* always being behind the counter. I knowed their old rule…"

"Knew."

"Beg pardon, ma'm, but it's an *old* rule, not a new one, about there being somebody at the counter, *all* the time…"

Hepzibah Sharpe snorted. "Elsie, what's the point?"

"So, I just went around the counter—I'm thinking they never heard the bell—and when I went behind the counter, I could see their back room…"

"Elsie, I do not need a map. What happened?"

"There's a bunch of people in there, and *they're telling Miss Winifred she can't be matron any more!*"

Hepzibah grabbed Elsie by the apron and yanked her into the carriage. If she had hoped for thanks, the hope was wasted.

"Listen here," said her mistress, "and listen carefully: ride in this carriage with *her*"—she pointed to Elizabeth, and handed Elsie the end of the green sash—"to Scrapebottom Cottage. Leave the urchin with Lettie, then go to Sharpe Corners, up to my room, and pack me a traveling bag with clothes for at least three days. Be sure to include my ermine stole and my black bombazine. Understood?"

Elsie gulped, nodded, then made the tactical error of speaking, "But ma'm, I couldn't get your package."

"You idiot, we have more important cakes to bake!" hissed Hepzibah.

"Cakes? Baking?" said Elsie, puzzled.

"I was telling you, there are more important things to do!"

Elsie, obviously confused, changed the subject. "Ma'm—what if Miss Lettie's not home?"

"She's always home. The important thing is to keep this girl away from Sharpe Corners, so Lettie will simply have to take her in." Hepzibah made this pronouncement as she stepped out of the carriage. Turning back, she issued one more ultimatum. "Have my bags waiting by the side door in an hour. And...one more thing: you must make sure and certain she sees *no one* and talks to *no one*, or I shall be extremely angry and will take my displeasure out of your wages!"

Elizabeth would have made use of the time this conversation took to escape from the other side of the carriage but for Hepzibah's sash. The edges cut into her wrist, and she was trapped. But when Miss Sharpe stepped out the door, Elizabeth's foot was free enough to kick her loose shoe, which hit the bricks on Market Street with a *thwack*. The carriage pulled away, and she heard the bell over the Feathergill's door for what she was sure was the last time.

# CHAPTER THIRTY-TWO

*Hepzibah to the Rescue*

The shop bell clanged as Hepzibah Sharpe entered Feathergill's with a firm tread. She sidestepped the counter without a glance as to whether or not anybody stood behind it, steamed into the meeting like a battleship, and smacked her handbag down on the table.

"Excuse my late arrival," she said with all the air of someone who had actually been invited. "My maid informed me of your doings, and I came to speak for my sister, for I am her aide in all things pertaining to St. Gumbert's. Her intense affection for the place and for the dear orphans" — she paused to cough — "prevents her from defending herself well. She is an excellent administrator, but perhaps a poor speaker."

"The Havershams," said the president, "left us a most convincing letter..." He pushed the document down to Hepzibah, who absorbed the contents, then scanned the table for a crack in the wall of the Board's stern attitude. Finding an overdressed lady in pink who seemed sympathetic, she focused on her and proceeded.

"Well, I must say that Wallace and Lydia could have been here if they had something to say. But I am perfectly happy to answer your questions," she said, although "perfectly happy" was not the phrase an observer would have used for her expression. She pressed her lips together and pulled at the pointed fingers of her moss green gloves. Moving her mouth into the shape of a smile, she spoke.

"Dorrie is nothing but trouble, and my sister has been very, very patient with her. She admits she has little contact with the girls," she said. "Winnie has kept the little ne'er-do-wells off the streets and labored tirelessly to teach the wastrels to respect authority. All the countryside is better for the work she's done at St. Gumbert's. Dorrie sees almost nothing of the orphans."

"The schoolmistress who does, also signed this letter."

Hepzibah Sharpe drew herself up even straighter. "Think for yourselves, ladies and gentlemen: when, in the history of education, have children *not* complained about their school? Of course, the instructor blames my sister when the fault lies at the schoolroom door!"

"Well..." the board president faltered. "I suppose you have a point. But the claims from the merchants seem believable. We took it upon ourselves" — the gentleman in the purple tie looked around at the other Board members — "to write inquiries to local merchants, and they responded that they have not been paid in *over a year*."

Hepzibah Sharpe proceeded smoothly. "Surely you, of all people, know the difficulty of dealing with tradesmen. Tardy and unreliable, they fail to deliver what's ordered, and try to charge twice for the supplies that *were* ordered. Gumbertville is full of shady tradesmen who cheat us every time they get the chance. And, I would add that never once have we come to the Board to ask for extra money. Surely, my sister would have if she couldn't pay the bills."

The Matron, by this time, had roused herself enough to speak.

"Well, honestly, what do you expect people to say when you write and ask if you owe them money? Of *course*, they are going to say yes, in hopes of getting extra payments they don't deserve, snatched right from the mouths of our poor orphans! Really, these accusations are disgraceful.

"Local grocers and glovers and pencil-pushers are in a plot to take advantage of us!" Matron continued. "And that Dorothy O'Rourke is a sly creature. The only correct thing in her letter is that I have no replacement for her. If I did, she would be outside the walls by sunrise tomorrow. I do admit, I like good food..."

Hepzibah, sensing her sister might be doing more harm than good, interrupted. "Consider the food children love. That's what you'll find on the menu at St. Gumbert's. Noodles and frankfurters and cheese sandwiches, simple meals. They wouldn't eat caviar if we served it, and my thrifty sister wouldn't waste the Board's money trying!" She smiled.

The board president's spade-shaped beard waggled as he spoke. "The Havershams thought the accusations had merit. The Havershams thought the charges were serious. The Havershams thought there were plenty of reasons…" he faltered again and looked to the other Board members for support. "They seemed to think we should relieve you, Winifred Sharpe, of your position as Matron of St. Gumbert's."

A look that could only be described as cunning passed across Hepzibah Sharpe's face, although her sister seemed frozen in place.

"Please, let me answer on Winifred's behalf. Of course, Wallace and Lydia have been gone a long time, and they aren't as familiar with the challenges of running the place as the six of you are." She paused artfully. "They've made a suggestion—but must you follow it? I'm sure there are areas where Winifred could improve—speech-giving, for one—but these charges against her have no foundation."

Mariah jumped into the discussion. "But what about the girls not being allowed to play? About them only going on to be servants and maids? I am here today, in a good position, one that St. Gumbert's prepared me for. Do girls now have the chance I had?"

"But you were exceptional, Mariah," said a lady in bold green silk stripes.

The plump lady in pink seemed anxious to change the subject. Turning to Matron, she said, "I do know you've always given us every impression of efficiency." The other five members of the Board nodded as if they were marionettes controlled by the same string.

Matron spoke into the awkward pause.

"You chose me, years ago, because I run an efficient establishment, not one that mollycoddles girls and allows them to fall into the trouble they are naturally prone to. I remind you that you have always expressed your pleasure in my management."

Hepzibah Sharpe added, with another one of her smiles, "And really, Winifred has had very few young ladies of Mariah's caliber to work with."

Mariah did not appear happy to be flattered. She continued, "I graduated from St. Gumbert's twelve years ago, and Agnes, Beatrice, and Candace came a few scant years after me, but there seems to have been a terrible change."

"That's all well and good for you to say, as an opinion," said Mr. Ludlow, his beard waggling again. "We all have a right to our opinions. But it's just your opinion that things have changed. You haven't been there, and we *have*. The Havershams haven't been there, and they aren't *here*, either.

"What about Agnes, Beatrice, and Candace? They are all from St. Gumbert's, and they are all exceptional young ladies."

The Board members looked at each other, uncomfortable and confused. One or two of them coughed; the ladies shifted in their seats. A wordless agreement to change the subject again seemed to take place.

"Well…" one said, "I think we should consider the many years she's been our Matron…"

"And the fact that this is all based on one short letter and only two missing orphans we know about *personally*…" said the lady in bronze.

"Not to mention the excellent dinners we are always served when we come to inspect…"

The meeting was going terribly wrong, thought Mariah. She looked over her shoulder once more before speaking.

"One of those 'missing' orphans is our pride and joy, here at Feathergill's, and she is supposed to be here to tell you what it's like now. She *escaped,* goodness knows, and what very little I've been able to get her to tell me confirms what the letter says. Life at St. Gumbert's, for her, was awful.

"Agnes, Beatrice, and Candace are out looking for her right now."

For reasons that will be obvious to the reader, Matron's face paled. Hepzibah Sharpe, however, looked smug.

The Board president smacked a wooden yardstick on the table as if it were a gavel. "So, *you* lose orphans, too, here at Feathergill's? This is not the Matron's problem, but a problem of having hooligan orphans who won't stay put! I say we have a Board vote as to whether the Matron stays or goes. How many say 'stay'?"

The vote was six to zero, and the two Sharpe sisters sailed out of Feathergill's like parade queens on a float.

# CHAPTER THIRTY-THREE

## *Enough!*

Elizabeth might have been able to get Hepzibah Sharpe's belt off her wrist if she had really tried. Elsie the maid was too worried to pay her much mind, and the carriage door was not locked. But the world looks different when a person has no hope, and Elizabeth, at this particular moment, had none. *I'm not wanted anywhere, and I have nowhere to go,* she thought.

Meanwhile, Elsie was formulating what she would say to Miss Lettie when they got to Scrapebottom Cottage. This was wasted effort, as things turned out, for nothing she could have said would have persuaded Miss Lettie to take Elizabeth in.

"I've been pestered and prodded about taking in an orphan, over and over, for years and years," she snorted, standing in the crooked doorway that gave into her dilapidated kitchen. "And Hepzibah gets all high-and-mighty, every time, without once offering help. And she got very nasty with me when that little chit you have with you ran away. So, you can tell my sister Miss Bossy-Bustle that I've…had…ENOUGH! There, I've said it. ENOUGH!"

With this pronouncement, she slammed the rickety door in Elsie's face. (And, let us note here that Miss Lettie crossed another threshold when she said the word "enough." Enough. That day it entered Miss Lettie's vocabulary, and if this story had been about her, we would go on to tell our readers that her life improved quite a bit after she learned to use it. But it's not, so we move back to the scene in the carriage.)

Poor Elsie didn't have an idea what to do. She was a very literal-minded girl, which meant, in daily doings, she did *exactly* as she was told without doing one bit less than was asked, or one bit extra. This worked well, if you worked for Hepzibah Sharpe. But Elsie had no resources when she couldn't follow instructions. And she knew from painful past experience that, when something went wrong, it was only a matter of time before she got in trouble. Life at Sharpe Corners felt like one long game of "pin the blame on Elsie." The game was no fun.

The carriage climbed the hill out of Miss Lettie's hollow to the back entrance of Miss Hepzibah's estate and pulled up under the portico. Elsie shivered as she got down and helped Elizabeth negotiate the carriage steps.

"The day's getting cold," said Elsie to no one in particular. "And I'm as sure as sure I don't know what's to become of *you*, or of me, for that matter."

She led Elizabeth, who didn't resist, in through a tiny vestibule, then through a dark hallway that seemed to change direction every ten feet, and which was jammed with boxes, trunks, and little tables. Elsie, accustomed to the clutter, dodged side-tables and low-hanging light fixtures expertly. Finally, they emerged into the kitchen, where Elsie did the only thing she had been able to think of.

She opened a door and yanked on the sash tied to Elizabeth's wrist.

"I'm putting you in here, 'cause you won't see nobody in a root cellar, and that's my instructions." And with that, she gave Elizabeth a shove down the few steps and shut the door behind her.

# CHAPTER THIRTY-FOUR

*A New Friend*

Elsie lost no time heading upstairs, where she could have been seen piling prickly garments into a capacious trunk. The job wasn't easy, since most of Miss Hepzibah's clothing had sharp edges, and handling them required gloves. The process was like packing broken glass. We'll leave Elsie to her task.

Meanwhile, back in the root cellar, Elizabeth looked around. The small, brick-lined room had shelves on all four walls holding crocks of onions, apples and various root vegetables, some large bins and sacks for flour and corn meal, and bunches of dried herbs hanging from the rafters. Under more normal circumstances, Elizabeth would have felt at home. A small window set close to the ceiling provided some light. She found an old wooden chair in a corner and sat.

Her thoughts were a jumble. The pain of believing she wasn't wanted crowded out her usual resourcefulness. Thoughts of a future at St. Gumbert's rushed in, and even worse, stretched ahead as far as her mind's eye could see. In this dismal state of mind, Elizabeth sat for quite a while. Then one tiny thought worked through the gloom: *Keep up your strength,* came the words, barely a whisper. Elizabeth got up and put an apple from a basket into one of her apron pockets. She wasn't hungry, but it would be wise to have something set by, she supposed.

A faint scraping sound startled her and turned out to be a key in the lock. The door opened. Elizabeth, her eyes accustomed to the dim light, saw a shape that might have been a lady or an angel, but that she somehow knew was not Elsie or Hepzibah Sharpe.

The shape was motionless for a moment, perhaps adjusting to the low light, and then spoke.

"Goodness my gracious, who are you?" said a voice with its own music.

"Who are you?" Elizabeth countered, cautiously.

"Well then, I'm Susan, and would you please come out of the cellar and have a muffin? I'm baking."

In the late afternoon light, Elizabeth saw a slender lady in a tattered gray dress, frayed at the collar and cuffs, with stripes on the shoulders where sunlight had faded the material (Elizabeth had seen that kind of fading on some of the dresses — the ones with narrow waists — that hung in the far corners of Matron's wardrobe, back at St. Gumbert's).

Without a word, Elizabeth stood up and went into the kitchen, with the stone floor and a black cast iron stove. A smell of cloves and allspice hung in the air. Susan motioned her to a chair at a battered table. She set down a plate of muffins and a butter dish, dropped a small slab of butter on a steaming muffin, and placed the plate in front of Elizabeth who, suddenly famished, took a big bite.

"I do the cooking here. Lettie and Hepzibah tell me I'm a relation, and I'm getting better after being sick for a long time. Heaven knows, the kitchen needed attention.

"So, that's what I do," Susan continued. "Can you tell me how on earth you came to be in our root cellar?"

Elizabeth swallowed. "Elsie locked me in. They're taking me back to the orphanage."

Susan stood in silence for a moment.

"And, what's your name?"

"Elizabeth."

"That's a lovely name. Do you *want* to go back to the orphanage?"

Elizabeth just looked at her, and her meaning was not lost on Susan.

"You don't have a family?"

"No," said Elizabeth.

"You don't have a home?"

"I thought I did, but I was wrong." Elizabeth's voice was a whisper.

"Then you're a lot like me. Hepzibah lets me stay—she says I'm a cousin-twice-removed—but that's not real family. I do the cooking to pay her back for taking care of me while I was ill. I've only been up and out of bed for a month or two."

Elizabeth, sitting in front of a drafty window, shivered. Susan got up and took a midnight-blue cape from a hook by the door.

"This house is always cold. Here, wrap my cape around you. I suppose Elsie was just doing what Hepzibah told her?" By now, Susan had gotten a tin lunch pail from a shelf and plopped more muffins inside. She seemed to be thinking, but looked up long enough to see Elizabeth's nod, then continued. "Four, five, six…and then there's some leftover ham"—she stepped to a tall oak icebox and removed a chunk of succulent-looking ham, which she laid atop the muffins in the tin.

"There," she said. "Hold on to this box. We must see what we can do. I can take you to live with me in the tower. Hepzibah has promised to find me some help. In the meantime, this box supper will be handy. Hepzibah's eating out, so we won't have a sit-down meal here, and you'll need something."

Elizabeth could have explained the flaws in this plan, but she never got the chance. The hall door swung open, and the doorway framed Elsie's horrified face.

"Oh no no NO!" she exclaimed. "You have to go back in that cellar RIGHT NOW!"

But she was too late. At the opposite side of the kitchen, the back door opened, and in that doorway stood the Sharpe sisters.

The only person in the room who showed no distress was Elizabeth's new friend Susan. "Hepzibah, you know how you've been meaning to find us kitchen help? Elizabeth here would fit in splendidly and spare you the trouble of taking her to an orphanage. She can share my room and be no trouble or expense to you."

Elizabeth, knowing more about the circumstances than her new acquaintance, was perhaps the most surprised person in the room when Hepzibah Sharpe paused, then answered while forming a smile, "Why, Susan, what a novel idea, one we must surely consider." She rubbed her green-gloved hands together. "As a matter of fact, my friend Mr. Smith is waiting under the portico. We could all drive downtown in his motorcar and get little Elizabeth a proper maid's uniform. Of course, you should come along...after all, you haven't been out in years. Why don't you go get one of my capes, since the child is wearing yours. Elsie, help her find the alpaca one with the frayed edge from my spare closet in the tower. Run right along."

Susan looked slightly startled, but she turned to follow Elsie. Then she turned back and spoke to Elizabeth. "It's going to be all right, you'll see. I'll be right back. *Keep up your strength.*"

No sooner had Susan and Elsie left the kitchen, and their footsteps were heard on the stairs, than Hepzibah Sharpe looked at Elizabeth. "You may go right ahead and get in the car with Mr. Smith. Winifred" – she looked meaningfully at her sister – "help her into the rumble seat."

What happened next is distressing to tell, but when Winifred Sharpe and Elizabeth, still wrapped in Susan's cloak and clutching the lunch pail, left the kitchen by the back door, Hepzibah immediately left by the hall door and hurried to the base of the tower stairs. She took a ring of keys from her pocket and shut and locked the tower door. She headed to the car with a satisfied smile.

162

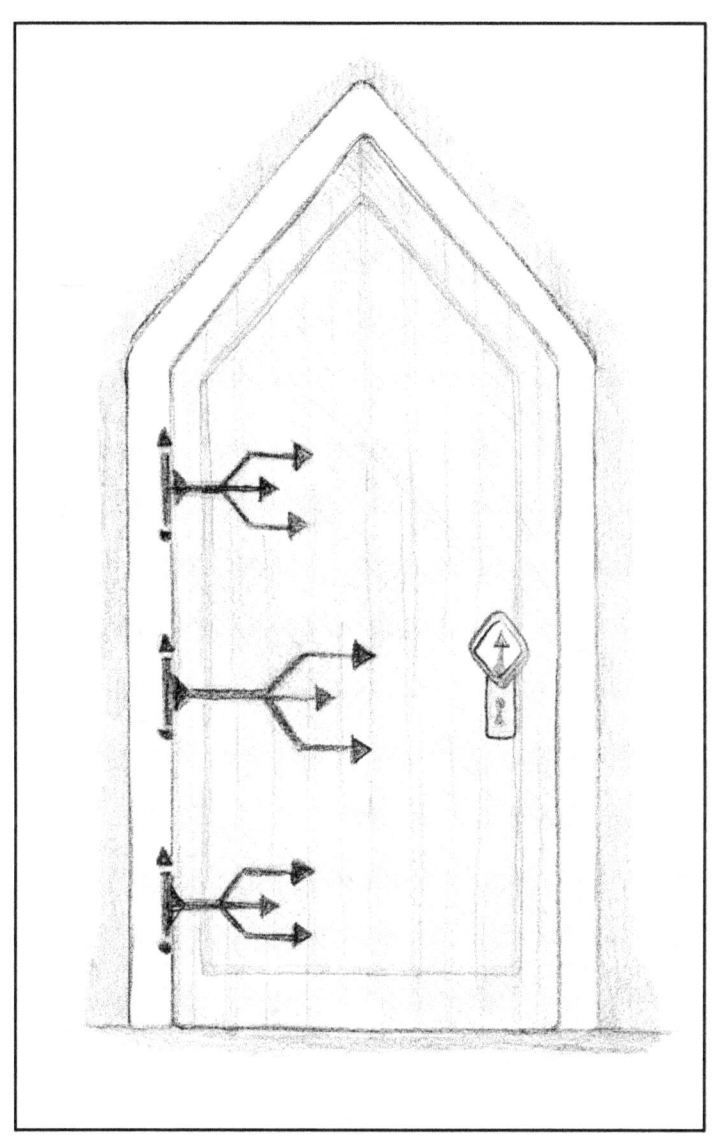

# CHAPTER THIRTY-FIVE

## *The Clue of the Shoe*

Mariah found herself barely able to be civil to the departing Board of Governors, back at Feathergill's Emporium. The Sharpe sisters may have sailed out the front door like parade queens, but the board members behaved more like confused sheep. They groped about for their bags and gloves, bumping into each other, murmured questions about the next train, and generally seemed unable to look either Mariah or each other in the eye.

Minutes after the bell over the door had signaled their departure, the Emporium held only the staff.

If you knew Mariah, you would have known she was upset. The Board members were too absorbed in themselves to notice, but Agnes, Beatrice, and Candace could tell. The four of them stood around the counter.

"We looked in all her favorite places, plus the train station," said Agnes.

"Nobody's seen her," said Beatrice.

"Not even Peabody," added Candace.

Mariah twisted her hands together.

"Where can she be if she's not with Peabody, not in her room, not at Pinkney's? She never got the thread she went to get. She didn't return when I told her to. Two hours have passed, and I'm worried to a tizzy." She jumped to the window at the sound of wheels on Market Street, but the rumbling was only Henry Greene's cart.

Beatrice started to speak, but Mariah, staring out the window, went on. "And I've failed the Havershams. Winifred and Hepzibah Sharpe pulled the wool over the eyes of the Board members, and I couldn't think of anything I could do."

"Without 'Lizbeth, and without Havershams, I don't see as there was much you could've done," Agnes remarked, matter-of-factly.

"I know, and anyway—me feeling bad isn't going to help us find her. Excuse me." Mariah straightened her shoulders. "I'll make a few calls on the telephone—I know the Havershams won't mind the expense—while you go and search again."

The three girls headed off in three different directions. Mariah picked up the telephone receiver and asked the operator to connect her to Wesley the sculptor. To her relief, he answered on the first ring and agreed to come at once.

Standing vigil at the shop window, Mariah saw Wesley stride up Market Street and pause in front of Feathergill's. He bent over and stood up with one small black patent-leather shoe in his hand. Mariah rushed out.

"It was in the crimp between the street and the sidewalk," said Wesley. "Not visible from the window."

"That's Elizabeth's," said Mariah. "I'd know it anywhere. And..." she seemed to pause to catch her breath, "and, in the *exact spot* where Hepzibah Sharpe's carriage was parked." Mariah's eyes narrowed, and her mouth settled into an uncharacteristic firm line. "Our Elizabeth was right outside the whole time, and those two unscrupulous spinsters *knew, held her there,* unless I very much miss my guess, while we all sat around and listened to them spin their spider-web excuses!" Angry tears formed in the corners of her eyes. "They're out to turn her into a slave or a servant. Hepzibah's been in, more than once, bothering her. The pair of them are *evil!*"

"Stay calm, Mariah. We'll be more help to Elizabeth if we're thinking clearly. I'd say our next step is to head out to Sharpe Corners. Where else could they take her?"

Just then Beatrice turned the corner from Parade Street. Mariah breathed a sigh of relief. "I'm so very glad to see you, Bea. Stay at the counter and answer the telephone, please. Write down any messages with particular care. Wesley has found Elizabeth's shoe, and we're taking the cart out to Sharpe Corners to look for her."

Wesley and Mariah found the gates of Sharpe Corners wide open, a circumstance unusual in Mariah's experience. They drove the Feathergill's cart down the winding drive, tethered the pony, and approached the front door. No amount of pounding produced a response.

Mariah looked worried. Wesley made a suggestion.

"This is no time to take no answer for an answer," he said. "If you catch my meaning. Let's walk around."

At the side of the house, under the portico, they knocked again, and again got no response, although they did observe a large leather travel trunk standing by the door. They proceeded to the back and pounded on the kitchen door.

There was no answer, but there was a noise, and then faint voices could be heard crying "help!" Mariah and Wesley looked around, then back toward the garden, then finally, up. They backed several steps away from the house, looked farther up, and only then could they see Elsie peering out a third story tower window.

"Help! Is that you down there, Miss Mariah? It's me, Elsie. Miss Hepzibah, she must've locked the tower door, on accident I guess, and she's gone and went off with that Mr. Smith in his auto-car, and like I said, the door's locked, and me and Miss Susan, we can't get out, and it's *cold* up here!"

At this point in the adventure, Mariah had an inspiration. "Elsie, is there a cellar door?" As an aside to Wesley she mentioned, "Those are often unlocked."

"There *is* one, Miss Mariah," said Elsie, doubtfully, "but Miss Hepzibah told me not to ever use it, no-how." Elsie went on, "…on account of because she didn't want the help stealing her apples."

Mariah rightly considered this didn't merit a response. She located the cellar's trap door, pulled the handle, then stepped into the opening. Wesley followed, and together they crossed the brick-lined basement and climbed the stairs to the kitchen. From there, Mariah knew enough of the house's layout (from previous visits to fit Hepzibah Sharpe's more special garments) to locate the door to the tower.

However, the massive oak door was locked, no key to be seen. There are doors that could be kicked open or broken down, but this was not one of them. Wesley and Mariah stood on one side; Elsie's and Susan's voices could be heard on the other, with Susan saying, "We'd escape through a window, but there aren't any on ground level. And I think Hepzibah carries her keys with her."

The sound of her voice, however, had the effect of inspiring Wesley. He produced a sculptor's mallet from his smock pocket and tapped on the door's hinge pins until, one, two, three, he got them out of their sockets, and the door creaked open on what had been the hinge side.

Elsie and Susan stood at the bottom of the circular staircase rising into the tower. Wesley stood in the doorway, and when he saw Susan, he stepped forward, and they fell into each other's arms. Elsie and Mariah looked on in some surprise.

# CHAPTER THIRTY-SIX

### *A Ride in the Suggsmobile*

We're glad we won't need to describe Elizabeth's trip in Simon Sugg's car in much detail. A rumble seat, in case you don't know, unfolds from the trunk of an automobile in motorcars at the time of this story, around 1910 or 1911. Rumble seats are not known, if they are known at all, for comfort. Simon Suggs's was worse than your average rumble seat, being backwards-facing and open to the air. Please remember, the month is December. The weather had been warmish when Elizabeth left Feathergill's that morning but had gotten colder and colder as the day went on. Close to freezing by dusk, with a promise of snow in the air, and Elizabeth and the Sharpe sisters were shoe-horned into Simon's small motorcar, which had two seats under the roof, and two places (it would be generous to call them "seats") in back.

"You can forget about that box of yours," Simon had said to Hepzibah when he saw the leather trunk Elsie had gone to such pains to pack, sitting by the side door at Sharpe Corners. "Because it won't fit unless it takes *your* place. What little space I've got, I need." Hepzibah Sharpe's face made it clear she was unaccustomed to not getting her way, and she gave the umbrella jammed between the two front seats a malevolent glance. She maintained a chilly silence until the car was well away from Granger's Green.

Suggs, lost in his own thoughts, never noticed his passenger's offense, and began to talk. "That maid of yours, Elsie, says Feathergill's makes cloth out of *words*. Words! And they're free. Free! I'm thinking, and planning, I'll build my own version, but mine will make lots and lots of the same fabric. I'll sell it at a nice mark-up and make an even nicer profit. And..." he smiled smugly, "I have the plans to show me how." He looked meaningfully at his umbrella, wedged between them.

Hepzibah Sharpe bit her lip and held her tongue. What she might have said would have caused Suggs to turn the car around, and she was in a desperate hurry to get to St. Gumbert's.

But she, at least, got to sit in the enclosed part of the roadster. Her sister Winifred and Elizabeth were pressed into the open rumble seat, out in the icy air, through the six-hour trip. Winifred Sharpe, whose cloak had been ruined when Elizabeth fought her way free, caught a nasty cold, but Elizabeth, whatever other problems she might have had, was actually snug, wrapped up in the cloak Susan had given her, a garment that seemed to generate its own warmth.

Elizabeth felt the drive would never end. The need to stop and change a flat tire, to correct a wrong turn that left them stranded in a frosty pasture, to wait while Mr. Suggs pushed the car out of a ditch and turned the crank to restart the engine, delayed them considerably, not to mention stopping for gasoline at Mr. Wallerton's filling station — these were just some of their delays. At least they provided time to eat the lunch Susan had packed. (Elizabeth stayed in the rumble seat through all these misadventures, due to having only one shoe.) The good food sustained her and helped her keep up her strength. Matron snorted and refused when offered a muffin.

The worst moment of the trip, however, was arriving. Elizabeth, who had fallen into a fitful sleep, opened her eyes to see the gray stone walls and the ramshackle gatehouse of St. Gumbert's Orphan Asylum receding from her gaze. Receding, because the car had gone through the gate and was inside, headed toward the main house. She was back. Would she ever get away?

They pulled up to the front. The Matron unfolded herself from the rumble seat with some of the same trouble you'd have unfolding a broken umbrella. To restore circulation in cold limbs, she stamped her feet on each of the front steps as she ascended, while fumbling at her waist for her keys. The stamping and jangling were the only sounds cutting through the cold December night.

Hepzibah Sharpe grabbed Elizabeth by the wrist and hauled her out of the rumble seat, marched her up the steps without regard to her missing shoe, and thrust her through the massive door Matron had just unlocked. The hall clock chimed ten times. Matron sneezed. Before Hepzibah could slam the door, Suggs erupted from his car, bounded up the steps, and stuck one sharply pointed shoe in the doorway.

"My tank's about empty. Do you have gas here?"

Matron rattled her heavy key ring and located an oversized skeleton key. "This unlocks all the outbuildings and the back gate, so bring it back *promptly*. You'll find the gardener's gas can in the shed."

Without so much as a thank you, Suggs jumped back in his car and chugged away. A surprise awaited him, about which the reader will learn soon.

Hepzibah Sharpe's tiny supply of patience was as low as Suggs's tank.

"Winnie," she said, annoyed at her sister's slow progress. "Hand me the keys. We must get to the office and grab the books. Before anyone sees them. We may have pulled the wool over the eyes of that dimwitted Board of Governors, but we are not going to fool anyone who gives careful scrutiny to the accounts."

She turned to Elizabeth and pointed with a key.

"And *then* you, missy, go to the Punishment Room. Mr. Suggs and I have a new plan. You go to his factory tomorrow. If you could work at Feathergill's, you can work for Suggs. Many orphans are already there— unwanted ones, like you. Simon always needs laborers."

Matron looked up. "Really, Hepzibah? She is a little young."

"She's old enough to cause a huge amount of trouble, and we cannot afford to have her here!"

The two Sharpe sisters, marching Elizabeth along between them, moved through the silent entry hall with the massive pillars, across the dining room, and down the back hall to Matron's rooms.

Everything was dark and quiet—the orphans were long since in bed. But a sliver of light showed below the office door.

# CHAPTER THIRTY-SEVEN

*Meanwhile, Back at the Emporium…*

We have been so absorbed in Elizabeth's problems that we have ignored other important people in the story. The Havershams and Peabody haven't been heard from since Tuesday morning, and by the time the Sharpe sisters returned to St. Gumbert's, it was late on Wednesday night. Clearly, explanations are in order. We'll need to go back to explain Sir Wallace's whereabouts, and him doing an irresponsible thing like skipping out on the Board of Governors meeting. After all, if he had been there, the Board surely would have fired Matron, and maybe Elizabeth might not be kidnapped. Speculation is dangerous, but still, we clearly require a new chapter.

Peabody had bounced out of his basement like a bagel from a toaster, bright and early Tuesday morning, catching the Havershams as Sir Wallace was about to drive Lady Lydia to the train station.

"I hate to be a botheration, but I have a thought about our prob-len."

Sir Wallace paused in the act of pulling on his driving gloves.

"What's up, Phineas?"

"It's about that Smith fella, the one who stole our plans. Our Elizabeth told me—I forgot till just now—his real name is Simon Suggs. He was masker-faking as 'Mr. Smith.' He runs a factory in Albertville, where a bunch of St. Gumbert's girls are slaving away makin' uniforms! Thought you'd want to know."

Peabody subsided.

Sir Wallace looked up. At that moment, he changed his plans. He decided to travel to St. Gumbert's with his wife, because she might need protection. And that they should drive rather than take the train, because they would need the car. And that Mariah could handle the Board of Governors meeting. Sir Wallace emerged from this train of thought to look at Peabody.

"Excuse me, Phineas, but I need to see Mariah…"

He stepped into Feathergill's and made apologies to Mariah, explaining that he would miss the Board meeting, set for the next day.

"Lydia and I are leaving you with an unpleasant responsibility, which will, no doubt, be awkward. But the Board has our instructions, and if Elizabeth tells her story, there's no answer to that. But Peabody has brought something to our attention that demands we investigate without delay. Lydia had planned to go alone—she wanted to see what the orphanage was like without Matron—but I have an idea something dangerous is going on. And if we're successful…" He paused, "the mystery of the extra word-dust and dying word-plants may have a solution."

# CHAPTER THIRTY-EIGHT

*Two Interrupted Journeys*

The Havershams climbed into their green roadster and were headed through town when they saw a lone figure, poorly dressed and burdened with a suitcase and a bulky box, standing uncertainly at the corner where Market Street intersects the lane behind the train station.

"Slow down, Wallace," said Lady Lydia. The stranger shaded her eyes and looked east, then west, as if uncertain of her direction. The Havershams observed a winsome face surrounded by curls barely contained by an out-of-season straw hat. Low summer shoes peeked out below a threadbare coat. Although the day was not especially cold, the stranger shivered. Sir Wallace stopped the roadster. "Can we be of help?" he asked.

"I wonder if you could direct me...to Feathergill's Emporium," were the words the Havershams could make out. The young woman swayed a little as she spoke, and Sir Wallace leaped out of the car to steady her.

"We'll give you a ride," said Lady Lydia, and the newcomer nodded as they helped her settle into the tufted upholstery in the back seat. Sir Wallace stashed her luggage while Lady Lydia covered her with a carriage blanket, soft and cozy.

"Wallace, we've got to get her warmed and fed. This young lady is weak, and her coat is thin as a hankie. We can't ask Mariah to do anything else today. I have another idea..."

The Havershams, always good at looking after people in distress, made arrangements and, when their new acquaintance was well situated, turned around and headed west toward St. Gumbert's Orphan Asylum.

Meanwhile, at dawn that same Tuesday, Matron had embarked on a rare excursion from St. Gumbert's. She left Dorrie in charge with a string of strict instructions.

"Make sure they get their work done. Make sure they don't get into my private cupboards. Don't answer calls from merchants, and don't go into the office," she barked. Two of the older girls stood beside her, and Dorrie thought they looked scared.

Matron stood in front of the huge hallway mirror and straightened her feathered hat. Gathering a pair of black kid traveling gloves from the marble-topped table, she turned to leave.

And the doorbell rang.

When Dorrie opened the door, there stood Malice Suggs, a chubby index finger still poised over the bell. "You took your time!" she exclaimed, hoisting a carpet bag over the sill and pushing her way in. She faced Matron.

"We have trouble at the factory."

Matron's mouth made a dissatisfied twist, and she slapped her gloves back down on the table. "I was coming to bring you help."

"The last help you sent *is* the trouble. We need to talk."

Matron turned aside to Dorrie. "Bring a pot of tea to my office." Turning to Malice, she gestured down the narrow hallway. The two older girls were sent to sit on a bench by the front door.

Half an hour later Matron emerged, frowning, and summoned Dorrie. "I'll be gone for two days, maybe three, and I expect to find everything in order upon my return. Oh—and if the butcher calls again, tell him his check is in the mail."

She made an impatient gesture to the two older orphans, and they all climbed into a taxi waiting outside. Malice Suggs, with her carpet bag, got in last.

Matron was almost never away overnight. Dorrie stepped back inside the big front door and tugged at a stray wisp of her curly hair. She took a deep breath, then headed straight to the kitchen, where she found Cook staring, Mother-Hubbard-fashion, at an empty cupboard.

"The grocer hasn't delivered in a week, and we're even out of dried beans, which is what I always serve when nothing else is on hand, and I surely don't know what I'm supposed to do for supper."

"This place has to change," Dorrie began, "and if you ask me, you and me—and Nancy, over in the schoolroom—can make the changes. We've got two clear days, maybe three. Who knows what we can accomplish? I wrote to the Havershams, and maybe that'll help. If not, I'm out of a job. But we need to *do* something."

"Well, I'd say it's about time. I can't make bricks out of straw any more in this kitchen," Cook had replied. "We don't have food in the pantry, at least, no good food, most of the time. No meat, no butter, no fresh veggies...and my sister flounces around on her high horse, eating her delicacies brought in special. Won't listen to a thing I say." Cook found her red stool and plumped herself down. She was not accustomed to standing and talking at the same time and found it something of a strain.

Dorrie stood still and stared. "Matron is your *sister?*"

"I don't go about shouting the news," Cook remarked. "We came here together twelve years ago, and things were different, back then. Was a nice place, was St. Gumbert's. Might've been an orphanage, but it was an orphanage with *heart.* No wall, nor did we need one! Since then, something's come over Winifred. She's changed, and I'm tired of being under her thumb, I am. I may not be much of a cook, but there's not anyone who could feed fifty growing girls with what I'm given." She folded her hands in her lap and regarded Dorrie. "Where do we begin?"

Dorrie said, "We could turn this place upside down in the time we've got. I want to search for food and better clothes for these girls. Their uniforms are a disgrace." She paused to think. "Why do we have acres of space we don't use? Why do we need a wall? Why is the upstairs locked?"

Cook became more silent than usual.

Dorrie shook herself and returned to her list of tasks. "I'll send a telegram to the Havershams, so maybe, if they're minded to, they could send help when Matron gets back, otherwise you and me are both out of work."

She continued, "And, do we have anything special for breakfast? Something besides gruel? Let's feed them TREATS."

Cook took a deep breath and eased herself off the stool. "Well, if Winifred's gone, then Winifred's special larder is fair game, I should think," she said as she shuffled across the kitchen to a locked cupboard she opened with a key. Inside were ingredients for a pancake breakfast, and some apples to cook up alongside. A gallon of maple syrup that had been stored in the cellar for special use by Matron was brought out, as well as an aged ham, and by the time breakfast was over, both had been used up.

Dorrie made a speech to the girls, who responded in heartening fashion. "Think of a treasure hunt," she told them, and who wouldn't love a treasure hunt? They started in the kitchen and explored cupboards no one had opened in years. They searched the closets in the hall and the shelves in the pantry, where they found extra blankets and fancy spices and cloaks and umbrellas from long ago. Nancy the schoolmistress pitched in, and girls took turns leading songs. There was a good amount of dressing up and play-acting, and Nancy even managed to work in some lessons.

After a couple of hours, Dorrie, who had been ransacking the kitchen cupboards, noticed a hook from which hung a large key. "What's this?" she asked Cook, who held it in her hand, an elaborate brass key with an ornate top.

"No one's been up there, not in years," said Cook.

"Been *where*?!" asked Dorrie.

"This…" Cook hesitated. Dorrie folded her arms and tapped her foot. Cook continued, "…is the key to the third floor. No one's been up there in years. Winifred won't allow it."

"Well, Winifred's not here," said Dorrie, stamping the foot she had been tapping. "If you ask me, we should go up and have a look-see. Maybe there's treasure for the girls!"

"Too many stairs for me," said Cook. "I haven't been up there since…well, never mind. But I'll be here, seeing about lunch. I think Winifred has some more supplies I can use for a good egg-scramble, and maybe the gypsies will help. We can work a trade with them—food for some of the treasures we've found."

So Dorrie unlocked the double doors to the third floor, and did a tour. Just as Cook had said, no one had been up there in years. (Well, except Elizabeth, who had long ago discovered a secret door in the ceiling of the second-floor linen closet, and that if you climbed up the cupboard shelves, there was a trapdoor that let you out in the third-floor hallway. So, Elizabeth could have told her what she would find. She also would have told them why she never went back up: the place felt *sad*. But Elizabeth wasn't there to ask.)

The third floor was like a museum. Dorrie and a few orphans who trailed behind saw beautiful bedrooms, outfitted with sumptuous curtains and bedding under vaulted ceilings, alongside bathrooms with patterned tiles, sculpted porcelain fixtures. All sat dusty and unused while, downstairs, the orphans had been sleeping on folding cots in a drafty dormitory after bathing in cold water.

Dorrie was, in her own words, fit to be tied and madder than a wet hen, if anyone had asked HER. And this is where we bring the Havershams back into the story. (The drive from Granger's Green only took four hours in their comfortable roadster, with no mistaken detours, flat tires, and breakdowns.)

# CHAPTER THIRTY-NINE

### *Like a Spanking*

Dorrie was just coming down the main stairs when the Havershams pulled up in front of the orphanage at noon, that Tuesday. Her greeting was unlike anything Sir Wallace had experienced, he said later. At least, not since he was eight years old and had been spanked soundly for stealing peaches from a neighbor's tree. That was, he said, pretty much how Dorrie's greeting felt.

"Let me tell you, that young red-headed lady marched out the front door and down the steps to our car. She made a brief curtsey, but I could see her fingers had a tight grip on her apron, and the first words out of her mouth were, and I quote, 'So you are the high-and-mighty Havershams?

Well, let me say that if you ask ME, I'd call you the Have-NOT-ershams! Because we have an orphanage here full of girls who do NOT have enough to eat, or wear, or learn! All in a house full of riches and plenty, all these years! And wherever you Havershams have been, it has NOT been here, where you were needed! And what I'd like to know is, what do you propose to DO?"

Sir Wallace and Lady Lydia had explained their twelve-year tour of the world and the trust they had in the Board of Governors, that they had gotten good reports while they were away, but after a while, they looked at each other, then at Dorrie. Sir Wallace stepped forward and said, "Miss O'Rourke, you are in the right, and we are in the wrong. We did not tend to our responsibility. We trusted our trustees without doing the diligent things that would have told us the true state of affairs at St. Gumbert's. We are heartily sorry, and we will make it right. Will you help?"

And Dorrie had been mollified. She turned around and gave them a tour, taking them through the mansion from the cellars to the attics. In the cellars—plenty of room for root vegetables, and potatoes, and all sorts of food that could keep dinner plates full, but the rooms were empty.

The Punishment Room made everyone shiver.

On the main floor—large and formal chambers, full of well-dusted and highly polished, unused, furniture. The kitchen—Cook's domain, with an empty pantry. A locked door—"That's the way to Matron's rooms and the office," said Dorrie. Then, up the main staircase to the second story. The library, and room after room that could have been used as bedrooms for the girls but weren't. The dark turn-off to the dormitory. Then, back up another stairway to the third floor with sumptuous, dusty chambers and an air of sadness.

When all had been toured and inspected, the Havershams understood Dorrie's anger. They stood, stunned, in the front hall.

Meanwhile, the orphans could feel the start of a new era. Lady Lydia ordered a feast from town. The Gumbertville Inn sent out fried chicken and crispy potato wedges and tray after tray of apple-pan-dowdy. Lydia would have liked to convert the uniforms into rags then and there but couldn't because the girls had nothing else to wear. And that's when she had a brainstorm. A call was placed to Feathergill's, where she had a long talk with Phineas Peabody. (Lady Lydia did not worry about the cost of long-distance phone calls.) Another telephone call, and a promise to pay an old bill, and the Gumbertville hardware store delivered twenty brooms. The girls swept up the dust that covered everything on the third floor and stuffed what they gathered into large canvas bags. Then Sir Wallace sent them out to play games.

Lady Lydia sat, deep in thought, on a bench in the entrance hall, looking at the locked door to Matron's apartment. After a while, she got up and sought out Cook in the kitchen.

"You haven't yet been in the office, I reckon," said Cook. "I see what you're doin', and I think I've kept quiet long enough. You'll be needin' to see the office if you really want to help and want this place to change. I have a key."

She trundled through the dining room and down the narrow passage beside the stairs. She stopped in front of an ornate carved door. Pulling out a large key she remarked, over her shoulder, "You can only get to the office through Winnie's quarters. Never mind the mess." The door opened with a creak.

Matron's taste, apparently, ran to gargoyles and gewgaws. The unwary person who got past the rooms she had stuffed with tipsy tables topped with china gnomes and lamps with fringed shades, still had to negotiate a narrow hallway lined with painted pots full of dead plants, then successfully duck a low-hanging ceiling fixture, dodge the arms of a spiky coat tree and only then, mostly in the dark, step around a whatnot table just to get to the office door.

Cook stalked through the clutter expertly in spite of her girth, bumping into only the empty tables and merely causing the cupid lamps to sway perilously. Lady Lydia followed, stepping carefully and feeling strong feelings about Matron's taste. Cook produced the office key with a flourish. "Winifred doesn't know I have this. I had it made, on the sly, one time when she took to her bed with a cold. The orphanage checkbook and some spare clothes are kept here. If I waited on her to open locked doors and cupboards for me, the orphans would have starved or frozen long time ago," said Cook.

She stood back and let Lady Lydia in.

# CHAPTER FORTY

## *Another Reunion*

The last we knew, Wesley, Susan, Mariah, and Elsie were at the foot of the tower at Sharpe Corners, late Wednesday afternoon. Wesley and Susan seemed to be old friends, but everyone's concern for Elizabeth had cut short their reunion. Wesley pulled Elizabeth's black shoe from a pocket and plopped it on the hall table.

"I found her shoe. Right where Hepzibah's coach was. I think they took her with them, wherever they went."

Elsie found her voice. She curtseyed, then spoke: "Well, yes sir. The little girl was with them, and I didn't know what to do with her, so I put her in the root cellar 'cause Miss Lettie wouldn't take her, no-how, and I wasn't supposed to let *anybody* see her. But Susan did. And I thought everything was fine, and then they locked us in the tower. Miss Hepzibah had me pack her a three-day trunk, so I know she meant to go away. I don't know about Miss Winifred."

Extracting facts from Elsie was like sifting gold nuggets from gravel, but some patient questioning produced another bit of information: the Sharpe sisters had been in contact with "that Mr. Smith, I think he was gonna drive them. He comes from Albertville."

This alarmed Mariah. "He stole Peabody's plans!"

Wesley, meanwhile, had rummaged in the hall table drawer and found a train schedule. "The train for Albertville leaves at five o'clock."

"Oh, but they're going to the orphanage," said Elsie, as if it was common knowledge. Wesley, frustrated, harrumphed. "Miss Winifred and Miss Hepzibah, they talked. They said they wanted to take that Elizabeth girl back where she belonged, they said. It didn't look to me like she was any too happy about it, either."

Wesley pulled out a pocket watch and said, "If we hurry, I believe we can catch the five o'clock express. But just in case..." He turned and picked up the phone. Elsie looked stricken and tugged his sleeve. She spoke with enough excitement to make her voice squeak.

"Mr. Wesley, you can't! Not nobody but Miss Hepzibah gets to use the telephone, Mr. Wesley! Miss Hepzibah, she'll have conniptions, she surely will! Her face turned real red when Mr. Smith used it, she was *that* mad! Please sir, hang up! She's most definite, it's a rule! Please, Mr. Wesley — send a note!"

Wesley didn't seem to hear. When the operator came on the line, he asked for the police and requested an officer meet them at the train station. Information was exchanged.

Wesley returned the receiver to the hook. He pulled some coins out of his pocket and pressed them into Elsie's hand. "This will pay for the call, but I think you may be done worrying about Miss Hepzibah's rules."

Wesley looked over her head at Susan. "You won't have time to pack. Let's grab the cart and leave."

Wesley, Susan, and Mariah ran to the pony cart and drove to the train station, where a policeman was holding the five o'clock express.

"I would surely make this trip with you," said Mariah. "but what if Elizabeth has escaped? After all, she escaped from St. Gumbert's to get here. And if she did, she'd come back to the store. And if she does, I ought to be there."

So, Wesley and Susan climbed aboard, and the train steamed away only five minutes behind schedule.

The journey from Granger's Green to Gumbertville took two hours by the express train. Thus, they arrived at the orphanage in a hansom taxi at seven thirty Wednesday evening. Dorrie opened the front door and gave the visitors an appraising look that took in Wesley's dirty sculptor's smock and beard, and Susan's frayed cuffs and the ragged hem of her gray dress peeping out from the worn edge of her outsized borrowed cloak.

"I think there's some good bits of leftover stew from supper. If you step around to the back," Dorrie began, "Just..." Well, truth be told, she was going to have them walk around the mansion, rather than let a pair of beggars inside, but changed her mind when she saw the weariness on Susan's face and the worn shoes on her feet. Dorrie beckoned and walked them through the foyer and down the servants' hall to the kitchen.

It took Wesley a minute to process what had happened, and when he realized they had been mistaken for hobos, he chuckled into a handkerchief pulled from his smock pocket.

Cook was washing up after supper, a hearty stew provided by the gypsies and paid for by the Havershams. She turned at the sound of footsteps on the tile floor, and when her eyes rested on Susan, she dropped an iron pot with a *clang* almost loud enough to be heard back in Granger's Green. To this day, the crack remains in one of the tiles.

"Land-a-goshen, if I believed in ghosts, I'd surely be seeing one! Miss Susan, I thought you were dead long years back, and here you are in my kitchen, large as life and twice as natural. I guess miracles still happen."

Susan looked puzzled. Just then one of Grimalkin's kittens skittered in, silver fur glittering against the black and white tiles. And Susan fainted. Fortunately, Wesley was nearby and caught her before she hit the floor.

# CHAPTER FORTY-ONE

*A Room Full of Secrets*

Let's see. Although the reader has been all over St. Gumbert's by now, we have not yet been inside the office, so it is only fair to put down a description. That we are not particularly eager to do so is because, frankly, the room is cluttered and crowded, much like the hall that Cook and Lady Lydia took to get there. Describing it will be a task, one on which we will now embark.

The office door would have led you to expect great things of the room on the other side. A relief carving of songbirds had been cut into a huge slab of solid oak, unusually wide, then hung on fancy brass hinges. No doubt the birds wished they could fly away from the dark hallway they faced on one side, and from the mess on the other.

Tonight, the door was already open when Dorrie announced Wesley and Susan's arrival. "We've got guests, and I guess Cook can vouch for them, and they say it's downright urgent to see you tonight, that it's about Elizabeth, so I thought…"

She never got to the end of her sentence, for Lydia Haversham jumped up and welcomed Wesley with a hug. He held her at arm's length in order to finally say what he had come to say.

"Elizabeth is missing. We think the Sharpe sisters kidnapped her. We think they're headed here. And I'd like you to meet Susan, who is my wife."

Good heavens, we have only gotten as far as the office door, and if we don't get right into our description, we shall never have another opportunity.

The reader has been warned about the mess. The orphanage office had had fine beginnings a century and a half earlier, as a dressing room for fabulous parties. The door had been made wide, the better to admit ladies in huge crinolines and gentlemen in heavily embroidered coats, lace cuffs, and powdered wigs, curled and pouffed. You could still see the flocked and filigreed wallpaper with white peonies set in gold medallions on a green background, and two built-in oak wardrobes, ornamented with vines and flowers. Carved crown molding kept the peace between the wallpaper and a ceiling on which was painted a sunlit sky and a flock of finely detailed bluebirds.

These elegant beginnings were overlaid with orphanage debris. Matron had the habit of thrusting unwanted paraphernalia here, everything from cracked crockery to torn bedsheets and broken umbrellas. The wardrobes held old uniforms and equipment for games no one was allowed to play. File cabinets stood at attention along the walls, containing the records from St. Gumbert's' beginnings back in 1880. A stack of damaged cots was jammed in one corner. Framed group photographs of each of the thirty graduating classes were strewn haphazardly on the walls, the last ten years piled on the floor, waiting forlornly to be hung. A bench was pushed against the wall by the door, and a few barrel-back chairs were sprinkled around the room like dandelions on an unmowed lawn. And the dirt! And the spiderwebs! Well, if you had asked Dorrie, something should have been done about them long ago, but neither orphans nor staff were allowed into this, the inner sanctum of St. Gumbert's. Only the desk near the door wasn't festooned with dust and cobwebs. A telephone and two leatherbound ledger books stood on the clean surface.

Wesley pulled up a chair for Susan near the desk, after wiping off the seat with his handkerchief. He stepped to the back of the room and stood like a sentinel in front of one of the wardrobes. Just then the office door bounced open, propelled by Cook's hip as she crab-stepped in with a tray, held aloft from having navigated the cluttered hall. Bowls of steaming gypsy stew and triangles of crisp buttered cornbread drew everyone's attention. She lowered the tray onto the desk after first clearing the account books from the top.

(The reader may be wondering why we'd slow down the action to mention how Cook put the soup down. The reader will be well advised to pay attention to little things like this—they might be important later.)

"What on earth are folks doing in *here*?" she asked, "There's no table space and no air. Stuffy places are bad for digestion. Folks need to keep up their strength," said Cook, handing the bowls around. All of a sudden, the room smelled of beef and bay and vegetables in tomato broth.

Sir Wallace, who had only arrived at the orphanage a few minutes earlier, was still removing his driving gloves. He slapped them down on the desk. "We're here because the orphanage accounts and records are here. Lydia and I have learned a great deal from them." He reached for a bowl of soup and seemed to be prepared to eat standing up.

Wesley held up his hand and repeated, "We have an *emergency*. Elizabeth is missing. We think Hepzibah Sharpe kidnapped her, and we think they are headed this way. Officer McDonald, back in Granger's Green, held the five o'clock express for us, so we were able to get here quickly. I hope and pray we are in time."

Sir Wallace set his bowl back down. "Dorrie, would your Tony be willing to keep watch at the gate?"

Dorrie left to find Tony. Sir Wallace, who had not eaten since breakfast, picked up his bowl. Dorrie returned with an update.

"Tony's at the gate, and if they drive in, he'll lock it behind them. The back gate's locked, so that should be okay." She added, "I think Matron has been shipping any girl she didn't like off to Simon Suggs's sweaty, stingy, slavery. It's flat out awful. And Malice Suggs gives me the willies!"

Cook, once everyone had a bowl, muffin-topped her way down into a chair. Dorrie paced back and forth in the few feet of clear space at the front of the room, her stew untouched on the seat of her chair.

"Cook is right. We should eat," said Lady Lydia. She resumed her seat at Matron's desk and took up her spoon. The rest of the room followed suit, except Sir Wallace, who put his bowl back down and picked up the telephone. He asked the operator for the police. In a few words, he outlined the situation, then replaced the receiver. He turned to face the room and cleared his throat. "If they bring our Elizabeth here, we're prepared. If they don't, the local police are on the lookout." He picked up his bowl and looked at Cook. "Thank you.

"And while we wait," he continued, "I think we could all benefit from some catch-up talk. Wesley, tell us how you found Susan. Your aunt and I had no idea you were married!"

# CHAPTER FORTY-TWO

*Susan*

"I met Susan, twelve years ago, while I was traveling the country. We married, but we've been apart for eleven years," Wesley began, "and I thought Susan was dead. We had an argument" — he coughed — "and Susan left. I traced her as far as St. Gumbert's, and I came here years ago, looking for her. The Matron..." he paused, then went on, "The Matron showed me a death certificate. Which I believed. By the way, are you aware the Board did *not* fire her this afternoon?"

"I had some doubts about how that would go," said Sir Wallace.

Wesley continued.

"I will tell you about the argument Susan and I had." He turned to Cook and Dorrie, "My full name is Wesley Wellington Haversham, and I come from Granger's Green. Sir Wallace is my uncle — my father's brother — and I grew up knowing all about Feathergill's Emporium." Cook nodded, and Dorrie made an impatient gesture that indicated he should move along. He continued.

"I was always inspired by what they did with people's words. I wanted to devote my life to doing something important with *my* words.

"Susan is a poet, and that is what I first loved about her — she, too, was in love with words." He took Susan's hand in his. "We each respected and valued what the other did, but...but, she would never listen to any good thing that I might say about Feathergill's. A strong prejudice against turning words into garments had been handed down to her through her family, and in my youthful enthusiasm, I could not leave the subject alone. I provoked a bitter fight, and my wife ran away.

"We've had a long talk on the train ride out here today, and I'm telling the story because Susan is only beginning to remember."

Susan spoke in her musical voice. "The first thing I remember is waking up in a tower bedroom. And a tall woman in a dress with metal trim told me I was a poor relation of hers, lucky to be taken in, and that I could do the cooking to earn my keep. I didn't know where I was. For years I didn't know *who* I was. I didn't remember I'd been married. Hepzibah Sharpe gave me to understand that I was her cousin, twice removed, and that I lived in her house on her sufferance and generosity after a long illness.

"Well, I like to cook, and I seemed to remember how, so I agreed. What else could I do? But about six months ago, late at night, I took to writing poetry, and reading aloud to myself, and sometimes to Elsie, in the tower room. And I found their old piano and remembered how to play."

Sir Wallace's face had an enlightened look. "About six months ago? Why, that would explain everything!" He went on. "Wes, I had the idea yesterday—because of the words piling up at Feathergill's—that, well, *someone* in Granger's Green was talking up a storm."

"That doesn't explain why the words wouldn't go into Peabody's pipe system, though," said Wesley, thoughtfully.

"I have an idea," Sir Wallace said, "...I made an important trip to the Gumbertville Town Hall this afternoon. I just got back. Everything revolves around Susan.

"Do you remember this place, my dear?" He directed the question at her.

She frowned and put down her soup spoon. "No. But Cook says she knows me, and I *know* I've seen silver-glitter cats before. I lost a great deal of my memory, but when I saw Wesley..." She blushed and continued, "I *do* remember him. My memory is coming back in bits and pieces. Apparently, I was very sick for a very long time."

192

Sir Wallace responded, "The missing pieces, Susan, are here in these records at St. Gumbert's." He gestured toward the file cabinets.

"Could Susan's plight explain Dr. Brown's ailing word-plants?" asked Lady Lydia.

"This all ties into Elizabeth's story. These office files held an admission form to the Gumbertville hospital under the name of Susan Haversham! Well! I went there, and I was told—hold on to your hats—six years ago, Susan Haversham was released to the care of Hepzibah Sharpe. But wait, there's more…"

Just then they heard footsteps in the hall and a scraping at the door, which opened to reveal Hepzibah and Winifred Sharpe, with Elizabeth wedged between them.

# CHAPTER FORTY-THREE

## *A Remarkable Gathering*

The astute reader will have noticed that many of our story's important characters are now in the office of St. Gumbert's Orphan Asylum or on the orphanage grounds, drawn there as if a team of storybook fishermen had reeled them in like so many trout. Of course, this is convenient for an author, but every one of them is there, late on Wednesday, for a compelling reason, and some of their stories are bound to come together.

Susan stood up and elbowed the Sharpe sisters aside, wrapped Elizabeth in a crushing hug and drew her into the office. Hepzibah and Winifred turned, and would have run away except the hall was so crowded with what-nots that both sisters fell headlong after tripping on the protruding leg of the coat-tree and each other. Wesley stepped past Susan and Elizabeth, grabbed the two Sharpes by their bony wrists and dragged them back to the office.

Susan found Elizabeth a chair. A general murmur of comforting words washed over her. "So worried about you!" "I felt so silly—letting Hepzibah trick me like that!" "So glad you're safe!" "So good to know you're in safe hands," and, "Thank God you're here," were among the many things said.

Wesley had the look of someone who has just remembered something, and he fished around in one of his capacious smock pockets for a moment before, with the air of a magician producing a rabbit from a hat, brought out Elizabeth's left shoe. He knelt down and slipped it on her foot.

Sir Wallace stood up. "Lydia and I think there are things that need to be said, mysteries that need to be solved, and some hearts that need to be healed. This Great St. Gumbert's Scandal needs to be cleaned up. It's handy that Hepzibah and Winifred have joined us. I will take just a moment to update the police." He picked up the telephone.

"We can keep 'em here tonight, sir," said Cook. "There's a room in the basement," she added, squinting at her two sisters, "…that oughtta suit just fine for an overnight. Seems about right. If a little girl got a night there for spilling a cup of milk, it should be just the thing for *kidnappers*." She crossed her arms and slipped into silence.

Matron looked shocked and pointed to the door. "My own rooms are just behind us. I am the Matron here!"

"Only because the Board of Governors, appointed by *us*," began Lady Lydia, "did not remove you, as Wallace and I instructed. I would advise you not to put a St. Gumbert's return address on your Christmas cards!" Matron grew pale, recalling that Christmas was only two weeks away.

Elizabeth looked across the room. Cook seemed embarrassed. She studied her fingernails. "My sister…" She stopped, and looked up at Matron, who frowned portentously. "Now look here, Winnie, there's no use you looking knives and daggers at me, and thinking up ways to be nasty when this is over, because it *is* over, anyhow. I hate being a cook, and I'm done pretending. I've gone along with your schemes and contrivances far too long."

Sir Wallace, still holding the telephone receiver, broke in, "It helps to know that Cook is the Matron's sister. There were four Sharpe sisters – Hepzibah, Winifred, Letitia…and Mehitabel."

"Cook's name is *Mehitabel*?" Dorrie exclaimed.

"She's Matron's *sister*?" squeaked Elizabeth.

"The Sharpe sisters always did have…interesting names," said Lady Lydia. "Their father was Zerubabble." There was no comment from the three Sharpe sisters present.

Hepzibah spoke up. "All Winifred and I have done is to bring an orphan back to the orphanage where she belongs!"

"Don't be ridiculous. The purpose of an orphanage is to find homes for orphans, not to steal them from a home they're in and keep them prisoner. We want Elizabeth back at Feathergill's, and one of the few things I know about her is that she does *not* want to return to St. Gumbert's," said Sir Wallace. He resumed dialing the phone. "I'm placing a call to the police…"

Every eye in the room turned toward him. The call went through quickly, but the result was not satisfactory. "What?!" Sir Wallace exclaimed. "When?" Then, more alarmingly, "Is anyone hurt?"

He hung up the phone and turned to the room. "There's been a fire. At Suggs's Utility Garments in Albertville. It's burned to the ground, but the girls got out."

That was when Hepzibah Sharpe made her move.

# CHAPTER FORTY-FOUR

### *A Get-away*

What no one had noticed while Sir Wallace was talking was Hepzibah sliding toward the door. She had inched away from her sister Winifred on the bench, and, as everyone watched Sir Wallace, she reached forward with her right hand and grasped the account books Cook had set aside. She then reached back with her left, twisted the doorknob, and slipped through the open door.

The closing made a *click*. Wesley looked up and saw the empty seat on the bench, gave a shout, and rushed to the door.

Which wouldn't open. Had it been glass—it wasn't—they could have seen the jammed tables and chairs and that spiky coat tree Hepzibah had piled outside, all lightweight individually, but unbudgeable together. She had made her escape.

Wesley saw the hinges were on the door's other side, preventing him from using the trick he had used on the tower door.

Sir Wallace examined the windows, but iron bars, installed by Matron to discourage burglars from getting in, were equally effective at keeping them from getting out.

"Perhaps we could break a window and shout till someone hears," suggested Lady Lydia.

"Could we make a battering ram out of the desk?" asked Susan.

"I hope Tony sees her," said Dorrie. "or she'll get away!"

Elizabeth spoke into the hubbub. "I know a way out."

Only Dorrie heard, and, with admirable presence of mind, put two fingers in her mouth and whistled.

The room went silent, everyone frozen in mid-action.

"Say that again, Miss Elizabeth."

Elizabeth repeated, "I know a way out. I can show you." And she walked over to the immense wardrobe in the back corner, pushed aside a pile of papers, and opened the door. Wesley joined her and helped move a collection of moth-eaten cloaks and three stacks of old towels and ruined uniforms. Elizabeth leaned in and hooked her index finger through a knothole in the wardrobe back and pulled.

The panel swung out, and beyond loomed a black hole. Elizabeth, without hesitation, climbed over the frontpiece of the wardrobe and stepped in, then looked back over her shoulder.

"The stairs go to the cellar. They go down, then come back up in the kitchen. We'll come out in the secret place by the butler's pantry where I keep treasures."

"I'll light a candle," said Dorrie and, suiting the action to the word, produced a match. Elizabeth led the way.

"I never knew about this! If I didn't know, then certainly no orphan should! It's against the rules!" Matron sputtered. "And, there's no sense hunting for Hepzibah, she's surely gone, with Simon Suggs. Let *her* have his rumble seat!"

Sir Wallace prodded her to move down the stone stairs.

Tony met them at the front door when they finally got out of the mansion. Dorrie's fiancé was a large young man who normally moved slowly, deliberately, but they could tell he'd been running. His blond hair was scrumbled, his cheeks were flushed, and his blue eyes looked concerned.

"Mr. Suggs," he gasped. "I think he's *dead!*"

He took a deep breath and continued explaining as they hurried to the front gate. "He wanted me to let him out, but of course, I wouldn't—I had your instructions. So, he started arguing."

Tony continued as they ran. "He said, *Open that gate!* and I said, *No deal,* and he said, *You'd better!* and I said, *Not on your life!* and then he up and tried to punch me, but his arm wasn't long enough, and I stuck my arm out, and, and, I'm telling you, I barely tapped him! But he bounced back against the gate house, and just lay there on the ground!"

Everyone ran harder. St. Gumbert's had a long drive. Before they reached the gate, they heard the unmistakable rattle-bang of the Suggsmobile with Simon at the wheel, waving jauntily as he drove away on the drive that circled the orphanage.

That's when Elizabeth looked up and, in the branches of her old friend the hawthorn tree, saw a blot, silhouetted against the full moon. Before she had time to speak, the blot became a downward streak just as Suggs's car passed underneath. The shape, accompanied by a squawk, landed in the rumble seat. The car continued at a reckless pace.

A flag of some sort stayed in the tree. Suggs' motorcar was out of sight – with Tony and Wesley, running hard, but still trailing behind by the length of a football field. In the light of the full moon, they had a view of Suggs unlocking the back gate and driving away.

They stopped, turned, and tramped back to the group. Everyone talked at once.

Dorrie asked, "How did he open the gate?"

"He had Matron's key," said Elizabeth.

"What is that, up in the tree?" Wesley asked.

"Looks like a flag," Sir Wallace replied.

"I'll climb up and get it," said Wesley.

"Wait!" Elizabeth exclaimed. "Not everyone can climb the hawthorn." She looked at Wesley appraisingly. "You *probably* could, but I *know* I can. It's magic." She ran across the lawn and clambered up in the branches, the spikes rolling up into balls obligingly, and retrieved what proved to be…

…Hepzibah's cloak, ripped and torn after getting the worst of her contact with hawthorn spikes. Elizabeth disentangled the garment and let it fall to the ground. Cook bundled up the shredded remains.

"I wouldn't be surprised," she said, "if this wise old hawthorn set a trap."

"There's a magic hawthorn back in Granger's Green," said Lady Lydia. "I never knew of another."

"I think," Cook continued, "the hawthorn made the climbing easy and the getting down impossible. But when Suggs came along, she slid down on her cloak."

"She might as well have flown off on a broomstick," said Lady Lydia.

"Hawthorn or no hawthorn, they've escaped," said Sir Wallace, "and there's no policeman in Gumbertville tonight."

Wesley noticed Matron backing away, and deftly took her by the elbow. By wordless consent, everyone walked back to the mansion.

They wasted no time getting Matron into the Punishment Room. Pajamas contrived from old uniforms were provided, along with a toothbrush and some cold water. We'll leave her there.

Although many questions remained unanswered and many stories remained to be told, the hall clock was now striking twelve—later than Elizabeth had ever been up in her life—and everyone was drooping with weariness. Dorrie was able to take them to the newly discovered rooms on the third floor. Wesley carried Elizabeth upstairs, and they all fell asleep as soon as they closed their eyes.

# CHAPTER FORTY-FIVE

*An Awkward Breakfast*

Early the next morning, two Gumbertville policemen, back from Albertville, arrived at St. Gumbert's. Only Cook was up and about. They took Winifred Sharpe into custody. She protested vehemently about her clothes; the police sergeant explained that she would soon be getting a prison uniform.

By then, the household was up. The officers listened to Sir Wallace as he told them about Simon Suggs and the stolen blueprints, Hepzibah Sharpe and Elizabeth's kidnapping. They were not terribly helpful. "I'm not sure we could arrest him," the officer explained. "Maybe he didn't know he was driving a kidnap car, and we don't know if he has your stolen plans. He wasn't anywhere near Albertville when the fire started. As far as we can tell, he's just a businessman. You could call the Albertville police — see if they can catch him with your blueprints."

As unsatisfactory as this was, Sir Wallace at least had the pleasure of seeing Matron led away, wearing handcuffs and makeshift gray pajamas.

Then the gypsies, who had, in the past two days, realized that providing orphanage meals could be profitable, came up with dozens and dozens of eggs and pounds of homemade sausage and bacon. Cook had only to provide stove space and table settings, and a general feast resulted. The orphans were seated down the length of the formal dining room table and were served.

Elizabeth rubbed the sleep from her eyes and washed, and dressed, in something of a daze. Susan and Wesley collected her from her room and brought her downstairs to sit between them at the table, a table Elizabeth hadn't seen since she'd helped Dorrie with table-setting, much earlier in this adventure. The room was full of orphans chattering about new possibilities at St. Gumbert's, on top of the clatter of serving dishes full of scrambled eggs and bacon clinking up against steaming platters of toast, multiple pots of jams and jellies. Cook had outdone herself on the satellite dishes.

Susan and Wesley, by contrast, seemed a little shy with each other. Lady Lydia leaned across to tell Elizabeth about Susan being Wesley's wife, and the news caused Elizabeth to smile. She wondered how she would feel if she found she had a family. The thought kept her quiet, but in all the hubbub, no one noticed.

After breakfast, she pushed back her chair and found Cook behind her. The orphans stared, for Cook never entered the dining room.

"Something I want to say to you, Lizzie," she began. "I want you to know, you're always welcome in my kitchen, and, well, I'd like to have you back." She turned to speak to Susan. "It goes without saying you could always come back, too. The years you worked by my side, well, they were good years."

Susan smiled, but made no reply.

"Thank you very much," Elizabeth responded, "but I need to go back to Granger's Green. They don't know where I am, and Mariah might be worried."

"I understand, Lizzie, but I thought you ought to know you have a home in my kitchen any time you want one."

Elizabeth felt confused and embarrassed. She stared at her shoes, then looked up and repeated, "Thank you." She didn't want to hurt Cook's feelings, but she didn't want to be an orphan again. She looked down and shuffled her feet.

Cook turned to go back to the kitchen, but Sir Wallace motioned her to stay. Breakfast was over, and Lady Lydia stood up to address the orphans. "Girls," she said, "this is a new day and a new life." She looked at Nancy, the schoolmistress, and said, "I wonder if you would take on the task of setting up a real school here, with advanced classes where they are needed, with lessons in music and art, with sports and cooking and training in areas where there's an interest. Sir Wallace and I will be back in a few days, and if you could, in those few days, put together a list of what you would require and how much help you would need, we will start classes in January."

Nancy had smiled her assent.

"And in the meantime, the task I would assign to everyone today..." She paused, and the room's mood hung in the balance. *Would this new arrangement really be better than the old one?* was the thought in many an orphan mind. Then Lydia continued. "Today's task, everyone, is to go with Tony to find the largest Christmas tree in the Gumbertville woods, set it up in the main hall, and decorate it from top to bottom!" A cheer went up from the table, and the girls tumbled over themselves (after being excused and clearing away the dishes, of course) to prepare for this excursion.

Wesley and Susan stood. "Susan and I would like to take a walk around the place in daylight," he said, and they made their way out. Elizabeth saw Susan give Cook one of her special smiles.

That left Sir Wallace and Lady Lydia, Cook, Dorrie, and Elizabeth alone in the big dining room. Elizabeth hadn't been face-to-face with the Havershams since Lady Lydia's visit to her room, back at Feathergill's, and she still winced every time she thought about that conversation.

Sir Wallace stood. He looked at his wife and said, "The time has come for explanations. But first, let's move to a more comfortable place." He led the way from the dining room, through the elaborate front parlor, and into a small sun room, where windows on two sides flooded the room with morning light. Cook followed, bringing a tray with fresh coffee and tea.

Lady Lydia picked up a bone china cup and sipped. Everyone chose a seat from the comfortable assortment of chintz-covered armchairs. Smiling at Elizabeth over the rim of her cup, she said, "I've been thinking back on this whole adventure. We almost lost you, Elizabeth! When you rescued

Charlotte Emerson, not only did you save her, but you rocked the foundations of this orphanage. You did some very brave things."

Elizabeth turned red, and wished they weren't all looking at her.

Lady Lydia spoke again. "There is another matter yet to be ironed out. Elizabeth, come here." She held out her arms, and Elizabeth, left with no other option, stepped forward, her heart pounding. Lady Lydia placed her hands on her shoulders.

"You were a help during a very busy summer at Feathergill's, stepping up to assist Mariah. She told me she was so glad you came." Lady Lydia took a deep breath. "Mariah said she watched as you were kind and generous while the toddler you rescued got a home and a family when you had neither. Thanks to you, that little girl became acclaimed for her artwork. Of course, I don't know what went on in your mind, but I can only say your behavior has been commendable, even noble, and your thinking, quick and resourceful. *You* got us out of the office last night!"

At this point, Elizabeth, very much to her own surprise, burst into tears. She didn't feel at all the way they seemed to expect her to feel. "No, I'm not! Please, you don't know—I lied about the castle book. It isn't mine, I stole it from the orphanage! And, and…I was so jealous of Charlotte, and, and…I'm so sorry…Please don't send me away!" Elizabeth cried hard.

Lydia hugged her. "There, there. You belong with us. Didn't you wonder why I was so interested in your baby ring?"

"I thought you thought I stole it," Elizabeth hiccupped.

"Nobody thought that, ever, or I'd've set 'em straight, straightaway!" exclaimed Cook, jumping into the conversation. "When are you going to *tell* her!?"

Lady Lydia turned. "The time will come," she said. Then, to Elizabeth, "You're no thief. And, to get back to your ring—look—I have one just like it."

Elizabeth looked at Lady Lydia and saw, on a filigree chain, a ring just like hers. The sight left her speechless.

Elizabeth looked up cautiously. She pulled the gold ring on its chain from under her collar. She found her voice. "This ring?"

Lady Lydia set her cup on a side table and said, "Yes. When I saw yours, my heart skipped a beat. I wasn't sure, but you see—your ring is the twin of mine." Lady Lydia held out her hand, and Elizabeth reached out to touch the ring.

"It's *exactly* like mine," she said.

"Let me tell you the story, Elizabeth. We've had to put the pieces together over many years from clues unearthed in all sorts of places. The story explains the link between Feathergill's Emporium and St. Gumbert's Asylum."

Lady Lydia arranged the folds of her skirt, cleared her throat, and began.

# CHAPTER FORTY-SIX

## A Runaway Sister

*A hundred years ago, two sisters lived in Granger's Green. One, I knew well – she was my Granny Lucy. Her full name was Lucille Feathergill. Her father founded Feathergill's Emporium, and she took over after him when she grew up. Her husband, my grandfather, built the mechanical works that Phineas Peabody manages today.*

*She gave me her baby ring, a ring just like yours, Elizabeth.*

*But this is the story of Granny Lucy's sister, Lavinia. Ten years older than Lucy, she was talented, beautiful, quick-tempered, and fascinated by fashion. Her angry words, made into cloth, came out as stiff and unyielding as she. The fashion in the 1820s was for soft, fluffy-ruffly shepherdess-style costumes, and Lavinia's word-cloth couldn't be made into anything like that.*

"Any more than you could make a bridal veil out of corduroy!" said Sir Wallace.

"Exactly," agreed his wife. She continued.

*Lavinia hated Feathergill's so much she ran away with nothing but the clothes on her back, her gold baby ring, and a wicker basket with her silver kitten. Lucy, only eight years old, missed her dreadfully.*

*She fled to Gumbertville, where she found work with a fashionable seamstress. Her family's pleading letters, addressed to Gumbertville General Delivery, went unanswered.*

*Lavinia worked hard and started her own shop where she could indulge clients with every latest trend. One such customer was George Granville, handsome but slightly vain, who came in for a satin waistcoat. He was the heir of the Granville fortune and the Granville mansion. Admiring her beautiful face and stylish clothes, he impetuously proposed marriage on the spot. She said 'yes,' and the wedding took place in the grand parlor here in this mansion, which was the Granville home.*

Elizabeth peered into the parlor. "St. Gumbert's wasn't always an orphanage?"

"Heavens, no. And, if you peek around the doorway, you'll be looking at the room where they held the wedding," said Lady Lydia.

Elizabeth did so and saw the parlor through new eyes.

Sir Wallace chimed in, "But it was a case of 'Marry in haste, repent at leisure.'"

Lady Lydia nodded. "Yes. Lavinia was a difficult person to be married to."

She picked up the thread of the story.

*They had two sons, Bostwick and Sedgwick.*

Elizabeth noted the name Sedgwick.

*As years rolled by, Lavinia embraced every fashion trend and oddity, even invented some of her own.*

*In the 1830s, she indulged her taste for the shepherdess styles she couldn't get from Feathergill's, with extreme flounces and sleeves puffed up like clouds in the sky.*

*In the 1840s, she took a turn into hat-making, and made headgear so large no one could make their way through a doorway.*

*In the 1850s, her gowns grew longer and as wide as Sir Wallace is tall, if you can imagine. That style was dangerous — the skirts caught fire with alarming regularity. And, above the waist, they were so tight the wearer could barely breathe.*

*In the 1860s, she invented what became a national sensation, the bustle, a contraption that formed a bump over a lady's, er, posterior.*

Sir Wallace interjected, "And a more ridiculous piece of clothing has never been devised, in my opinion!"

Lady Lydia smiled, and went on:

*"The invention took the fashionable world by storm. All the ladies of Gumbertville vied to be the first to wear it, even though the weight gave them back pain, and the pointy shoes that looked good with it made walking difficult.*

*Meanwhile, the two Granville sons grew up. Bostwick married. Not surprisingly, Lavinia picked a fight with his wife, who left the mansion, taking their baby daughter, named Elizabeth. Bostwick went with her, a decision that probably saved his life.*

Elizabeth noted the name "Elizabeth," and kept listening.

*For in the terrible year of 1878, a deadly influenza spread through the land and reached Gumbertville. George Granville brought the first case to town when he returned from foreign travels. Lavinia and George were quite old by then, and the flu was especially deadly for elderly people.*

Sir Wallace chimed in, "Young people don't understand, for nowadays we have a medicine, but fear gripped the heart of every person who could hear a deep cough or feel a fever on a loved one's brow. The flu of 1878 was a lingering illness; people were sick for weeks before succumbing. I remember it with horror."

Lady Lydia continued.

*In a way, this was a mercy to the headstrong Lavinia Granville. From her sickbed she saw her life clearly, and she longed to make amends. She wrote to Lucy, the sister she hadn't seen since she was eight years old.*

*Granny Lucy showed me the letter. 'Dear Lucy,' Lavinia wrote, 'I have been desperately foolish, wrong-headed, and unkind. All the high fashion in the world cannot replace family. Can you ever forgive me?'*

*Of course, my Granny Lucy wrote back. She wanted to visit, but it would have been too dangerous. She forgave her gladly, and the sisters were reconciled.*

Lady Lydia sat up in her chair with the air of having finished, then blinked.

"My goodness, I've forgotten Sedgwick! My second cousin..."

She resumed the tale.

*Sedgwick Granville, like his mother Lavinia, saw life clearly while suffering with the flu. Unlike Lavinia, he recovered. Resolving to track down his brother, he wrote to us in Granger's Green, asking us to take on the care of the Granville mansion and the Granville inheritance, so he could search for Bostwick, his wife, and daughter Elizabeth. But they had vanished without a trace.*

*He wrote that letter in 1879.*

*My father accepted the responsibility. He had the mansion fumigated, and all the drapes and hangings cleaned and aired, to ensure no infection lingered. Wallace and I were newlyweds, and we helped transform the Granville mansion into St. Gumbert's Orphan Asylum. We waited until no influenza had been reported for a year and then opened it as a refuge for girls left homeless by the epidemic.*

Sir Wallace explained, "Young orphan boys found new homes quickly. Farm families who had lost a son or a father needed help. Not so much, young girls. Lydia and I set up St. Gumbert's to teach girls everything they would need to know to become all they were put on this earth to be."

Lady Lydia finished the story.

*We cherished and nurtured the silver cats. Here and Granger's Green are the only places they appear. Just as only here, and Granger's Green, are magic hawthorn trees. I wonder if the seed from the Granger's Green hawthorn traveled to Gumbertville in the folds of Lavinia's cloak.*

*And Sir Wallace and I have traveled the world, continuing the search that Sedgwick Granville began for his niece Elizabeth. We found she had grown up, got married, and had a baby girl, but we never could trace her.*

Elizabeth found her voice. She had been counting on her fingers, keeping track of generations of relatives, then asked, "So the castle book, inscribed to 'Elizabeth, from Uncle Sedgwick,' was a present to...my grandmother?"

"That's exactly correct, my dear. And you are named for that very grandmother."

"How do you know?" Elizabeth asked.

"You have Lavinia Feathergill's baby ring, handed down to you through her son Bostwick, then to his daughter Elizabeth, then to *her* daughter, your mother, and then to you."

Cook leaned forward and interjected, "When are you going to *tell* her?"

Lady Lydia just smiled, held a finger to her lips, and moved on.

"And the book with the picture of the castle belongs to you, so you may certainly call it your own. I recognized it, up in your room. Mariah loved it when she was here."

Elizabeth hiccupped and raised her head. "*Mariah* came from St. Gumbert's?"

"Twelve years ago. Agnes and Beatrice and Candace came later. I knew them and asked them to help at Feathergill's. St. Gumbert's used to be a happy place. My goodness, there used to be art lessons and a traveling choir, and dancing instruction and cooking classes, and prizes for poetry and history. The grounds were beautiful, and there was no wall." Lady Lydia sighed. "Wallace and I have been away too long. Clearly, something went very, very wrong. I don't know what's happened, these past twelve years."

Elizabeth focused with intensity on one question: "So, you won't make me stay here, and you won't make me work for Mr. Suggs?" she asked, partly for the happiness of hearing the answer, because by now she was on the edge of feeling safe.

"Good heavens, no," said Lady Lydia. "*No one* will work for Mr. Suggs, ever again. And, dear Elizabeth, we only know about him and his factory because you came to Granger's Green."

# CHAPTER FORTY-SEVEN

## *Various Evil Doings*

Lady Lydia and Sir Wallace excused themselves and retired to the orphanage office. Dorrie and Elizabeth helped clear the tumble of furniture out of the hallway.

"It was clear as clear," Lady Lydia said. "Put bluntly, someone had been cooking the books. But Hepzibah's taken them, and without them, we have no evidence against the Sharpes." A frown made a home on her brow.

"I'd spent almost two days examining the orphanage accounts. Large amounts of money were missing from the orphan's general fund. Any accountant could see what I saw. The great shame is that no one had double-checked the records in *years*."

Dorrie got up. "I always thought there was something fishy about the money here. If you ask me, it's been going on for a long time."

Sir Wallace looked up and said, "Lydia will never say so, but she is a genius with figures, and bookkeeping is her specialty. The Sharpes reckoned without her — she saw through the holes in their records."

"And while she examined the orphanage accounts, I was over at the Gumbertville courthouse, examining a different sort of record book. I've been looking into birth certificates there, and adoption records here. We still have *those*."

He was busy moving papers extracted from the orphanage files to his valise.

"It didn't take an expert," said Lydia, modestly. "They had, apparently, been charging a fee for placing orphans, and pocketing the money. They had also been charging families whose daughters had been lost, charging extraordinary amounts of money to return the girls to their homes and pocketing the money. Elizabeth's kidnapping was, I think, not their first. A ransom scheme! Simon Suggs paid them a finders' fee for bringing him young ladies to work in the factory. And then, he had workers who didn't know they could do better elsewhere, because they'd never *been* anywhere else. Suggs paid his workers in factory money, so they could not leave.

"And of course, they cut the funds spent on the orphans to the bone, to the end that there was almost no food, or warm clothes, or school supplies, anywhere at St. Gumbert's."

"And all the money that wasn't spent on the orphans, ended up in Matron's, and Hepzibah's, pockets," Sir Wallace chimed in.

"Despicable," Lady Lydia intoned.

"Plain rotten," said Dorrie.

Just then Wesley and Susan burst into the office. "I thought," he began, "I'd call ahead to Feathergill's, to tell Mariah we found Elizabeth—but someone's cut the phone lines!"

"Suggs, I'd wager," said Sir Wallace.

Tony was not far behind. "I found the place outside the front gate where they're cut. If they'd just been snipped," he continued, "I might-could've fixed 'em, but there's a whole stretch of wire missing." Tony smiled modestly.

Sir Wallace shrugged. "They probably headed to Albertville, where the police will apprehend them."

The Havershams held a conference with Dorrie and the younger Havershams—Wesley and Susan. Tony, they decided, could stand guard at the orphanage in case Suggs and Hepzibah returned.

"I don't think he's coming back, sir," said Tony. He scratched his chin, and Elizabeth noticed the muscles in his arms. "I don't think he wants to see me again." Elizabeth pictured a fight between a sunflower and a daisy.

# CHAPTER FORTY-EIGHT

### *Two Different Automobile Rides*

The Havershams had planned to take Wesley, Susan, and Elizabeth to the Gumbertville police station in their comfortable motorcar. From there they would proceed to Granger's Green.

Plans do not always work out.

The drive to Gumbertville proved both impossible and unnecessary. Impossible, because Sir Wallace discovered the front tires of his automobile had been slashed. Unnecessary, because a tall, thin policeman met them at the orphanage front door.

"I'm Detective Carmody. The chief sent me out after he talked to the officers that came earlier. He read about the S.U.G. factory in *The Albertville Herald*, about bad conditions and girls too young for factory work, and the articles say those girls come from St. Gumbert's. Since the fire, they don't have a home, and we wondered..."

Lady Lydia didn't wait for him to finish the sentence. "Bring them here, please; we'll take care of them," she said. "I'll tell Cook and Dorrie." She headed to the kitchen.

"Our telephone lines have been cut, and our tires have been slashed. Suggs has escaped, along with Hepzibah Sharpe. We think they headed to Albertville," said Sir Wallace.

"Then there's not much I can do," the officer replied. "...if they're in Albertville. But I can help get your car on the road, and I can call the Albertville police when I get back to the station."

Well, Sir Wallace had one spare tire, which he and Officer Carmody changed, and Tony was able to patch the other. There was no immediate help for the telephone lines, but Detective Carmody promised to send a repairman.

So, Elizabeth had her first real ride in a motorcar, for we won't count her trip in Simon Suggs's rumble seat, which was facing backwards, unenclosed, and done in the dark of night. In the green roadster, in bright midday sunshine with fresh snow on the ground, she was given a seat beside Lady Lydia, and could press her nose against the window glass. The snow-covered scenery seemed to move past the car, instead of the other way around. Deer stopped in their tracks, and rabbits scurried out of the way, amazed at the vehicle's miraculous speed of twenty miles per hour. Inside, she was cozy, battened down with carriage blankets over tufted tan leather upholstery, and she didn't have to think about anything. She wasn't worried about Simon Suggs while she was safe with the Havershams. She wished the ride would last forever.

Another car, with other passengers, had made the trip toward Granger's Green the night before. Moving our story back a few hours, we find Simon Suggs and Hepzibah Sharpe on a very different journey. Villains have to do their business in secret and in the dark; it's the way villainy works. So of course, Hepzibah and Simon would not want the reader — or anyone else — to know what they talked about on that fateful drive. We have the information from a passenger they weren't aware of. When Simon was arguing with Tony, back at the front gate, an inquisitive chipmunk had hopped into his car and hunkered down on the warm floorboards.

When the vehicle drove off, the chipmunk no doubt thought he was embarking on a fine adventure. Imagine his surprise at the bump and thud of Hepzibah falling into the rumble seat, and his concern when Suggs stopped outside the gate to let her into the passenger seat. Wisely, the small creature said nothing, but huddled under the dashboard, awaiting developments.

Midnight snow was falling when they turned left from the orphanage lane onto the icy main road, unaware of the tiny stowaway. Before they had gone a mile, Miss Sharpe told Suggs of the fire at his factory. He stopped the car.

"My factory? *Burned down?!*"

"Correct. And the entire St. Gumbert's police force went to Albertville to help. I would add, I believe they mean to charge the bosses with setting the fire and putting the girls in danger." She gave him a piercing look.

"They can't blame me; I wasn't there!" he exclaimed.

"I'm sure I don't know. But going back to Albertville tonight might not be prudent. As a matter of fact..." She paused artfully. "There might be a better plan, for I am the owner of an empty factory..."

Suggs anticipated her thought. "I could start over, anywhere I choose. I *have* plans, the plans from Feathergill's! Never mind how I got them," said Suggs.

Interruptions offended Hepzibah Sharpe. She spoke, as she was prone to do, sharply, "Simple Simon, you have the plans that built Feathergill's, yes. But you need a building. And you don't know the secret lying deep below Feathergill's. My maid Elsie knows things you never saw on the tour her uncle gave you. The secret of Feathergill's..."

She told him about the plant cave. Then she added:

"No one in Granger's Green knows your name is Suggs. No one in Granger's Green knows my connection to St. Gumbert's. At least, not that they can prove, because I have the account books here with me. Let Malice take the blame for the factory fire, let Winifred take the blame for the orphanage. With my factory, you could start over in Granger's Green, make a great deal of money...and put Feathergill's out of business!"

"Great minds think alike, lady. I can cut my losses with the Albertville factory. The place was getting to be a thorn in my hide. Let Malice deal with the police—that woman could talk her way out of quicksand." He looked down the road with an expression that indicated he saw wealth on the horizon. "If I ran a factory with free cloth, like Feathergill's, I wouldn't bother with all the pipes and special treatment. No, I'd turn out yards and yards of gray canvas, easy-peasy. I'd hardly need staff."

He paused. "How about a partnership? I'll let you in on the ground floor, so to speak. We'll put Feathergill's out of business. Who needs their antique ways? I'd use modern methods, get modern results. I've got their plans. You've got an empty factory. And…"—he gave her a calculating look—"*you* know about these magic word-plants. Do business with me. You'll be better off without your stuffy sister. Clearly, you were the brains of the orphanage operation."

The conversation lagged as the car crept along the main road. Every once in a while, Hepzibah said they should go faster, and just as often Suggs snarled back that they couldn't, but otherwise, the only sound was the crunch of the wheels on the snow and the tinkle of the bits of metal that trimmed the hem of Hepzibah's ankle-length gown. (Remember, she had left her cape in the hawthorn tree.)

Their fellow passenger—the reader will remember the adventure-seeking chipmunk under the dashboard—took an interest in those pointy bits of metal. He climbed onto Hepzibah's shoe for a better look. Balanced on his tiny feet, he batted at the nearest doodad before beginning a climb up her stockinged leg, using his sharp little nails to grip the wool stocking—and the leg underneath it.

Oh, the shrieks! The flailing, kicking, and screaming! Honestly, this may be the only place in our story where Hepzibah Sharpe deserves sympathy. The reader might even have some to spare for Simon Suggs, who loved his automobile, which, when Hepzibah grabbed his steering arm, slid off the road and tumbled down an embankment, coming to rest upside down, its nose mashed against a tree.

Cars, back then, were constructed of thick, strong metal. Both Simon and Hepzibah were able to climb out of the wreck and walk away. Their small fellow traveler abandoned his designs on Hepzibah's decorations and made a new life for himself in the tree the car had crashed against. A squirrel family adopted him.

Suggs and Sharpe didn't have it so easy. They got back to the road, bruised, cold, and wet. Then they saw a light in the window of Fred Wallerton's place.

The Havershams' auto pulled up at Wallerton's filling station the following afternoon, the occupants ready to get out and stretch after the two-hour drive. Elizabeth even wondered if she might have time to build a snowman while they refueled and rested. But that plan, and any others, were quickly dispelled when Mr. Wallerton did not appear to pump their gasoline and could not be summoned by Sir Wallace's call at the cottage door. Lady Lydia noticed the door was ajar, and everything about the journey changed.

Why? Because, inside Mr. Wallerton's ancient stone cottage, in the midst of a surprising clutter of clocks and telephones, sat Mr. Wallerton himself, gagged and trussed up like a Christmas turkey. He struggled to speak, and Susan was quick to remove the handkerchief covering his mouth and eyes, while Wesley pulled out a pocketknife and cut the cords binding his wrists and ankles.

"Are you hurt?" "What happened?" "Who did this?" A series of agitated questions were asked, but Mr. Wallerton had few answers.

"I went to bed at midnight, heard a noise at two in the morning, and before I could so much as get my slippers on, something hit me, and that's all I know. I woke up tied up, and golly but I'm glad to see you!"

Sir Wallace had stepped over to the phone on the wall, but the line was dead. He frowned. "Mr. Wallerton, will you be all right without a telephone connection? I think your lines have been cut. We can bring you to Granger's Green with us."

"No, no, my place is here. I see you've got the fire going in the stove. I'll be on the lookout for trouble."

Sir Wallace assured him the police would be called; Wesley filled the car with fuel and paid Fred Wallerton. Everyone sat on the edge of the soft leather seats the rest of the trip to Granger's Green.

# CHAPTER FORTY-NINE

### *Return to Granger's Green*

Even with a twelve-hour head start, Suggs and Hepzibah reached Grangers Green only a few hours ahead of the Havershams. Their progress had been choked by the snowstorm, by the crash, by the time it took to bop Mr. Wallerton, tie him up and steal his pony, and then by that same pony's extremely slow gait. The two villains, bruised and battered, reached Sharpe Corners at nine o'clock in the morning. Hepzibah sent Suggs to the tower, while she had Elsie draw her a hot bath, into which she tumbled after having explained she did *not* want Elsie to draw her a picture of a bathtub.

Hepzibah would surely have spent the day in bed, for she was very sore, but Simon Suggs had Elsie summon her at noon, and the two of them departed in Hepzibah's carriage.

The two sets of Havershams plus Elizabeth arrived in Granger's Green closer to four o'clock that afternoon. Unlike Suggs and Sharpe, they were warm and dry upon arrival, but they were in a certain amount of distress caused by their discovery of Fred Wallerton.

"And," Sir Wallace added, "I'm suspicious of two phone lines being cut in one day."

"It does seem like the same person playing the same trick, not merely a coincidence," said Susan.

"Do you think Hepzibah Sharpe and Simon Suggs...came *this way*?" asked Lady Lydia.

"Let's see," Sir Wallace replied as he turned onto Market Street.

What met their gaze was the tower at Feathergill's, and the store door and window, festooned with Christmas ribbons and greenery, everything

222

frosted with glittering snow and highlighted by the red bricks showing where snow had melted. Shoppers thronged Market Street, and the scene could not have been more cheerful had it included Santa and reindeer.

Sir Wallace parked the roadster by the door, and Elizabeth tumbled out. Before she could so much as look around, the shop bell rang, and Mariah was running to greet her. Friends and acquaintances gathered. Hugs and greetings and introductions—no one at Feathergill's except Mariah knew Susan—were exchanged. Peabody emerged from his basement kingdom, the tinkling of his tools and oilcans as good as a brass band welcome.

Mariah wiped away a tear. "I was beside myself, worrying," she admitted. "And then we haven't heard a thing since Wesley and Susan got on the train!"

"The telephone lines at the orphanage were cut. We couldn't call," said Lady Lydia. She also explained, in a whisper, that Susan was Wesley's wife.

Then she continued. "We feel relieved. We were afraid Simon Suggs was making his way to Granger's Green, bent on harm and mayhem—but it looks like everything here is fine as could be hoped."

Mariah looked puzzled.

They were poised for a celebration until Peabody remembered Dr. Brown, and hustled downstairs to fetch him. Five minutes later he climbed back to the workroom, saying, "Something's not right, 'cause his cello is there, but the case is gone, and so is he! One thing I know—Exeter wouldn't take the case without the cello." He removed his cap and scratched his head.

Sir Wallace was more than puzzled, he was alarmed. A quick round of inquiries in the neighborhood did not turn up Dr. Brown.

# CHAPTER FIFTY

## *Sharpe Tacks*

Of course, people would have acted differently if they'd known for sure and certain that Hepzibah Sharpe and Simon Suggs were in Granger's Green. But they might just as easily have escaped to Albertville—perhaps the police there had already arrested them. Simon Suggs surely would have headed that way if he had any sense of responsibility for his factory.

Still, Sir Wallace had his doubts.

One obvious place to inquire was Sharpe Corners, so he headed there, taking Wesley along.

Elsie answered the door. She seemed confused. "Miss Hepzibah said to say she's not here, and that she hasn't been here. Mr. Suggs? I don't know any Mr. Suggs—did you maybe mean Mr. Smith? Well..." Elsie bit her lip and seemed to struggle for the right answer. "I'm not supposed to say he was here, either, so that's exactly what I'm saying, and there can't be anything wrong with that, can there?"

Sir Wallace framed his next question carefully: "Is there anything else they said you shouldn't mention?"

Elsie smiled, glad to be guided. "I shouldn't mention the tack factory, so I won't."

Sir Wallace smiled and gave her a pat on the shoulder. "Thank you, Elsie."

The old factory was no more than half a mile down the road. Old Zerubabble Sharpe, many years earlier, insisted on being able to walk home from work for his lunch, and had chosen the site for his factory accordingly. When Sir Wallace pulled up to the derelict building, he was surprised to see the police wagon, with Peabody and Chief Dogglemeyer. Peabody climbed down.

"I had a hunch to check this place," he said, gesturing beyond the building. "And Chief Dogglemeyer agreed. See the tracks and footprints in the snow? Someone's been here."

They made their way to the door and went inside. The old factory was one big open space, eerily silent. Patches of snow covered abandoned machines in places where the roof had rotted away. Tall windows in the brick walls would have given the feeling of a church, except abandoned black iron machinery rose up from the floor or hung down from the ceiling like spider legs reaching through the space.

With so much to look at, they didn't immediately see, seated on an iron bench in the midst of the machinery and mechanical debris, Hepzibah Sharpe. Peabody needed a moment to recognize her. She had one black eye and, upon getting closer, a bump could be seen over the other, just below the frayed edge of one of Elsie's knitted caps. Three heavy flannel nightgowns, worn because she was too bruised to get into any of her usual snugly fitted, sharply tailored, outfits, peeked out from under a lightweight, rhinestone-studded purple velvet evening cape. (The reader will recall that Hepzibah had loaned Susan her second-best cape and had left her best in the hawthorn.) One arm was in a homemade sling, and on her feet were unlaced boots that, it turned out, belonged to the gardener. Hepzibah Sharpe was a mess.

On the bench beside her sat Dr. Brown's cello case, overflowing with word plants.

Hepzibah stood. Her eyes were dull, but her temper was sharp as ever:

"You are trespassing, and you need to leave," she said imperiously. She turned and shuffled away.

The police chief called after her, "How does this cello case come to be here? Where is Dr. Brown?"

"How would I know?" She looked around. "Mr. Smith may have seen him, if you can find Mr. Smith. We're going to work together to refurbish this building..." She backed away. "...which will be good for Granger's Green. A new business. You'd be wise not to interfere with our plans."

But she had forgotten some things about her father's factory, for instance, the hole in the floor where rejected tacks had once been thrown. She fell in, with a squeal that hurt their ears.

Chief Dogglemeyer hastened to the shallow pit and, taking hold of her elbow, hauled her out. Her layers of flannel had provided some cushion, but she was in worse shape than before. He shepherded her to the police wagon, explaining that she was under arrest for kidnapping. Hepzibah seemed surprised, and if her injuries from the night before had not been so painful, might have put up a fight.

# CHAPTER FIFTY-ONE

### *The Great Stabberback Embarrassment*

Elizabeth was tired, and her stomach was upset from worrying about Dr. Brown. She wanted, more than anything, to go down to Peabody's basement kingdom, find MacTavish, and tell him her concerns. A purring cat on a lap can cure an upset tummy.

But when she got down the first flight of stairs—the ones that emptied into the huge room with the spinning spools—she stopped. She didn't know what to make of what she saw. For there was Simon Suggs, slung over one of the big spools like a dishtowel laid out to dry. Behind him stood Dr. Exeter Brown, doing something with the blue cord on the spool.

Elizabeth drew closer. Dr. Brown, she was now able to see, was tying Suggs's ankles together. The blue cord was already wound around his wrists.

"Ah, Elizabeth!" said Dr. Brown. "Your timing is perfect. I wonder if you might go upstairs and have Mariah fetch a policeman? I believe I can keep Mr. Suggs secure here until he arrives."

Mr. Suggs seemed to have a different opinion. He squirmed and yelled, which caused Dr. Brown to snug the blue cords and stuff a handkerchief in his mouth. "None of that, now," he admonished.

Elizabeth turned to go, then called out over her shoulder, "But, what happened?"

"I'll tell you more when Mr. Suggs is deposited neatly in the Granger's Green jail," came the calm reply. Simon Suggs made a sound like a growl. Elizabeth did as she'd been asked.

An hour later, everyone sat around Mr. Pinkney's best table being served hefty helpings of meat loaf and parsleyed potatoes. Dr. Brown told his story:

"That Smith fellow snuck into my cave, bringing a large canister of plant poison, stuff he'd gotten from Hepzibah Sharpe's garden shed. He threatened to spray all the word plants if I didn't give them to him, so he could start a new factory, using the plans he stole from Peabody.

"So, I seemed to help him. I dug up some of the younger plants—to my dismay, he put them in my cello case!—and off we went in the Sharpe buggy, out to her father's old factory. Hepzibah insisted on driving, even though she looked like a cross between a rag doll and a mummy."

Police Chief Dogglemeyer nodded. "We found her there, badly bruised. She said Mr. Smith, whose real name is Simon Suggs, was to blame."

"I believe they smashed Suggs's automobile on their way here last night. Then they stole Fred Wallerton's horse and rode the rest of the way. You'll find the nag—I mean the horse—in the pasture behind Lettie Short's cottage," said Dr. Brown. "Suggs talked fit to beat the band when we drove back from the factory. I told him his plants would die if we didn't get the plant food I keep here, and my cello. I confess, I fibbed." Dr. Brown smiled. "So, we returned to Feathergill's, and I diverted him into the spool room through the door off the back stairs. I knew Professor Longley was giving a lecture on the history of the flugelhorn this afternoon, so his spool would be filling up with nice, strong, fact-filled word thread. I tripped Suggs and used the professor's thread to snug him to the spool. I hope I didn't waste the Professor's words."

Mariah smiled. "There's not much chance the professor will ever be short of thread."

Police Chief Dogglemeyer blinked at the mention of the crashed automobile. "We'll investigate. But, with or without the stolen horse and the kidnapping, we'll put Simon and Malice Suggs in jail for a good long time. The way they ran that factory broke more laws than Pinkney's has pancakes."

"And I make a *lot* of pancakes," remarked Mr. Pinkney as he cleared empty plates.

Elizabeth, already tired, wasn't paying attention, so she was the first to notice Barbara Stabberback coming in, wearing a peevish frown and a dress decorated with arrows.

Peevish because she had been out of town all day, buying special custom undergarments. Upon her return, June Mooney had been quick to tell her all she had missed: the Havershams' arrival, Elizabeth's rescue, not to mention the talk-making arrests of Hepzibah Sharpe and Simon Suggs, and the astonishing possibility that Wesley and Susan were sweethearts. She shared that Suggs was really the Mr. Smith who had promised to make dresses that would cover her back. Never had Granger's Green seen an afternoon with so much news, and Barbara Stabberback had missed it all. A peevish look was the evidence of her distress.

Her path to their table was as straight as the arrows on her dress. "If this isn't a bunch of secret-keepers!" She began by aiming a watery squint at Wesley. "I can't help but wonder what you're doing here with *her*" — the glance singled out Susan — "when I *just* talked to June Mooney about her new book with a handsome sculptor-hero. How many girlfriends do you have, Wesley?" She gave a separate, malicious glance at Susan.

Wesley stared, dumbfounded. Susan just giggled. Barbara, disappointed at failing to produce rage or tears, went on. "And Peabody, your niece Elsie will be out of a job, what with Hepzibah Sharpe in jail. Where *will* she find work? She's not exactly the crispest chip in the bag."

"Mind your own business," huffed Peabody.

Unfazed, she forged ahead. "Maybe Elsie's competition is right here. Little Elizabeth will need a place to stay. Lettie Short can adopt her. Lettie always needs help. Elsie won't do. I'm surprised, Lydia, you haven't made arrangements."

"That's enough, Barbara," said Lady Lydia. She patted Elizabeth's hand. "And," she whispered, "not a bit true."

Mrs. Stabberback, satisfied she had done all the damage possible with what news she had, minced out of the restaurant onto Market Street. What happened next became the stuff of Granger's Green legend. From where she sat, all Elizabeth saw was a blur of orange, followed closely by Henry Greene. A series of thumps and squeals came from around the corner of Market and Parade. Curious, the party clustered at the window. In only a few minutes, Henry Greene reappeared, Marmalade sedately leashed at his side.

In years to come, he perfected the story of The Great Stabberback Embarrassment.

"Marmalade gets excited when he sees that woman and those laces she uses to cinch up the back of her dresses. Marmalade thinks the bobbles on the ends are toys. (He's such a frolicsome puppy!) She isn't nearly as happy to see him, I've noticed. Tonight, well, he gets a hold of one end of the string, playful-like. (He's very quick, is Marmalade.) That woman turns around and starts mashing at him with her purse in one hand, her umbrella in the other! Since she kept missing him, he thought she was fooling (A good-natured dog, that's our Marmalade). But, she flailed around, and he pulled back, and her laces…came undone. Woop! Woop! Woop! They slipped right out of their grommets, and *her dress front fell off!*

"Well, let me tell you…" This was an unnecessary remark, because everyone was riveted to the story. "Next thing I know, she spins around — but there was a patch of ice, and she trips and flops in the middle of Parade Street, then stands up with those black petticoats crusted with mud and snow, and Marmalade running in circles with her string in his mouth, like she was a Maypole. She beelines to Betty's Chocolate Shop, and there she stands in the doorway, clutching her petticoats and shrieking like a stranded seagull. You probably heard." Henry Greene paused, and a small smile crossed his face. "Marmalade followed—he's a very forgiving dog—that's when I came up and put him back on his leash. I must say, I wish we could separate Barbara Stabberback from her nasty talk as easily as Marmalade separated her from that ugly outfit."

Everyone nodded.

Just then Police Chief Dogglemeyer returned. "Amen. I picked up that nasty garment, averted my eyes, and handed it back. Wish I could arrest *her*. My day would be complete if I could. That tongue of hers stirs up half the trouble we see in this town. It's bad, but unfortunately, it's not illegal."

Henry Greene patted Marmalade's head. "I like to say, this dog is a fine judge of character."

The little group in front of Pinkney's window did their best not to laugh. Lady Lydia wiped a smile from her face. "Well, after the day we've just had," she said, "…we all need a little rest. But tomorrow is another day, and Wallace and I invite everyone to dinner at our house. A celebration. We'll send the car for you. Wear your best and prepare for music and a feast!"

That night Elizabeth, lying in bed in her tower room, thought all had gone well until Lady Lydia had mentioned wearing her best. *My best?* she wondered. You might have thought she'd have been excited about a party, but please remember, in only a day and a half, she had been kidnapped and rescued, trapped and escaped, starved and feasted, deeply insulted and highly praised. She felt dizzy, exhausted, perturbed. Her last thought before falling asleep was to wonder what she would wear to the party, since both her dresses were a patchwork of other people's cloth. And although she might not be headed back to the orphanage, did she really have a place in Granger's Green? If she did, wouldn't she have a dress of her own?

None of us do our best thinking when we're tired.

# CHAPTER FIFTY-TWO

### *A New Dress*

Sometimes a good night's sleep makes all the difference. Elizabeth woke up feeling bright as the sunshine twinkling through the frost on her window. A new day was dawning. She hopped up, washed her face, and brushed her hair. Her patchwork dress, hanging on the door hook, looked new. She ran her fingers along the meticulously stitched seams, each bit of fabric made of words, she thought, of someone in this town, *her* town. If she couldn't wear her own words, she could wear the words of people she knew and loved. She was *back* and wouldn't be sent away! She was back at Feathergill's, and they wanted her. She had new friends, some family, and no lies to cloud her judgment. She popped the dress over her head and smoothed the full skirt over her petticoat. For the third time in this adventure, Elizabeth had a moment of making up her mind. Deep down, she decided: whether or not Feathergill's ever made her a dress, she could surely be thankful for what she had. She went downstairs, eager to see Mariah and Peabody.

She swung around the newel post and almost skipped to the kitchen, looking forward to oatmeal with Mariah, Abigail, Beatrice, and Candace. Today, beside her bowl was a package with a folded card on top. The card said, "Welcome Home, Elizabeth." The package, done up in brown paper, tied with string, had a tag with *Elizabeth* in swirly writing. Her heart skipped a beat. She looked at Mariah.

"For me?" she asked.

"For you," said Mariah. "Finished an hour ago. The day before yesterday, Peabody came upstairs to tell me word dust had started to flow in your pipe, the one he built last spring! The jammed dust sitting in the sorting bin started to flow."

Just then, Peabody himself popped in.

Elizabeth reached toward the package, then looked at Mariah. "May I...open it?"

"Of course, silly! We're all waiting to see how you like it." Agnes, Beatrice, and Candace slipped into the kitchen.

Elizabeth untied the string and unfolded the wrapping paper, then the tissue paper. She saw blue fabric the color of an evening sky just after sunset, but before darkness falls. The color attracted her like a magnet attracts pins. The cloth was iridescent taffeta, woven into a surprising yet subtle plaid. Elizabeth let the folds fall out and saw a splendid party dress, exactly the right size. Holding it close, she spun around.

Then she stopped and asked, "But, what happened? Why wasn't there any fabric for me before?" She could feel her future hanging on the answer.

"There's an explanation," said Mariah. "Elizabeth, you're not from Granger's Green, so much of what you said, at first, got lost in Mr. Peabody's otherwise excellent system. You know he's had an onslaught of extra words—well, yours got mixed in."

"Funny thing," Peabody intoned, "the really funny thing is, your words look a lot like the words piling up in those canvas sacks. No wonder they were hard to sort. But somethin' happened yesterday, somethin' that let the sortin' bin figger out the puzzle."

Mariah went on. "But another issue came up after we got *your* words, Elizabeth, and made a place for your fabric frame—when we had almost enough material, all of a sudden a moldy yellow splotch showed up in that blue taffeta."

Elizabeth, dismayed, looked down at the dress.

Mariah smiled and said, "It's not there now."

"But why, on *my* dress?" Elizabeth asked.

Mariah answered, "Because of the book. The castle book. You said something, well, not quite true—"

"A fib!" said Peabody.

"And an untruth will always show up in your fabric. In yours, or anyone's. For some people, the fabric turns black, if they haven't been truthful. Some people's fabric gets splotchy white spots, and some people..." Mariah sighed, "some people tell so many lies their fabric just comes off the loom with blots all over. We do what we can, but it makes for an ugly garment."

"Fib-rot, we calls it. Nothing spoils fabric faster than a fib, we say downstairs, but we've all told 'em, 'specially when we get scared," Peabody interjected.

Elizabeth blushed crimson and looked down until Mariah reached over and, with a hand on her shoulder, looked her in the eye.

"My dear, let me tell you: every soul in town has had their cloth ruined by falsehood-mold..."

"Fib-rot!" Peabody interjected.

"...at one time or another. I have, Peabody has, all of us have."

Apparently thinking Elizabeth needed encouragement, Mariah went on. "I remember the time I let Hepzibah Sharpe get under my skin. She came in with her usual complaints, *and* a demand that I re-make her last two dresses, and I was so mad at her" — Elizabeth found it hard to imagine Mariah angry — "that when she asked for her new bolero jacket with the pointy buttons I'd cut my fingers on, I just told her she'd have to wait a week. All the while, the jacket was finished, and done up in a parcel under the counter. And I was *glad* she went away in a tiff. And then *my* new material came off the loom with a jagged pea-green streak of 'fib-rot'" — she smiled at Peabody — "cutting across on the diagonal. We couldn't remove the stain, and nothing worked until I went and delivered Hepzibah's jacket, and apologized. Her bad behavior didn't excuse mine. The looms know the difference. We learn our lesson when a good garment gets spoiled. You are not the only one who's told a lie, and you will not be the last. But Lady

Lydia told me you stood up and told the truth. Which took courage. And your stains disappeared.

"The lie is bad for the fabric, of course, but worse for the liar. All of a sudden, they don't know where they stand," she added. Elizabeth understood.

"It's like mixing sawdust into ice cream! Like tossing a cup of mud in the chocolate cake batter! Nobody wants a second taste. When people figger they been lied to, they stop trustin'. Makes for bad parties, bad neighborhoods, bad business. Causes prob-lens." Peabody was ready to go on but, at a look from Mariah, he cleared his throat and played with the latch on his toolbox.

"I think we get the point, Phineas," she said.

"One thing we know now, though" — Peabody looked at Elizabeth — "you belong in Granger's Green, and nobody no-how can say otherwise."

A weight lifted off Elizabeth's heart.

# CHAPTER FIFTY-THREE

*An Old Friend*

When evening came, Elizabeth, resplendent in her new dress, waited by the front door for the Havershams' car to come for her and Agnes, Beatrice, and Candace. Everyone looked their best, and everyone was excited.

Peabody emerged from the basement in a black swallowtail coat of a style no one had seen in fifty years, striped trousers, and a silk vest (he called it a waistcoat) embroidered all over with cunning lavender flowers. He was accompanied by a faint smell of mothballs and hair tonic, for his unruly head of hair, usually hidden under his cap, had been slicked into wings stretching out from a center part. He carried a battered red leather satchel. Elizabeth almost didn't recognize him.

"These here were me dad's embellishments," he remarked with a sweep of his hand indicating his outfit. "I takes 'em out of storage for special occasionalities. B'longed to my dad," he repeated. "Sometimes we wear our history."

The Havershams lived atop a hill east of Granger's Green, in a brick mansion studded with pillars and gables and chimneys. Elizabeth's first sight was through the motorcar's windshield as they rounded a curve. She felt dizzy, especially when Sir Wallace handed her out of the car and up the steps between massive pillars, wrapped in greenery and red velvet ribbons, to the front door. Elizabeth gasped when she saw who held it open.

Paulina! From back at the beginning of this adventure, glowing and pretty, well-dressed in a red frock with Christmas-green trim, a sprig of holly in her curly black hair. Elizabeth had never seen her look so fresh and lovely.

"'Lizabeth!" Paulina hugged her.

"Paulina! You're *here!*"

Paulina paused, then remembered she was standing in an open doorway on a December night. "Everyone, welcome and come in!" she called, ushering the party inside. There was a bustle while she helped them off with coats and scarves and gloves, and the Havershams came to greet them and hand out mugs of hot chocolate. When everyone had been made to feel at home, Paulina and Elizabeth sat on a cushioned bench in the foyer. She told her tale.

"When I saw you in the hall that night, I'd just found out Matron was sending me to Suggs's. I didn't know what to do. I'd heard it was awful, and I'd heard right. But the day I arrived, the strangest thing happened, and gave me hope. A mailman brought a package, for *me*. In the midst of a crowd of girls, waiting in the cold to get in the factory door at seven in the morning, he rode up on a motorcycle with a sidecar and found *me*. And handed me a big, heavy package. The return address was 'Feathergill's Emporium, Granger's Green,' and inside was a typing machine — they call it a typewriter. I took it as a nudge, a sign," Paulina continued. "A sign that I was meant to be more than a factory slave, that I should be a *writer*. And 'Lizabeth, I'll swear that mailman had wings.

"I started typing up stories like the ones I used to tell you at the orphanage. I sent them to *The Gumbertville Bugle*. Every time I'd finish one, that same mailman would just happen to be in the factory yard, and he'd take the envelope away. Good thing, for I didn't have money for the postage. And the newspaper took them and paid me! Then, I had the idea to write about Suggs! Well, they took that article and asked for more. And, they paid me! So, I saved up my money—Suggs doesn't pay a girl enough to buy a bootlace—and finally, I had enough for train fare to Granger's Green, where my typewriter came from. I couldn't go to Gumbertville, for they'd surely find me. So, I climbed out a window and walked to the Albertville train station, lugging my precious typewriter. But I was tired and hungry when I got off. I had just enough money for the ticket, with none left over for food! Well, the Havershams found me, just when I was about to collapse, and they took me in, so I could get my strength back…and here I am!

"And," she continued, "here you are, too! Lady Lydia told me. She told me what you did for the little girl, too. 'Lizabeth, I'm proud of you. Now, come see the house, and have a cup of punch. It's going to be a wonderful party."

# CHAPTER FIFTY-FOUR

*The Havershams' Party*

Now they were all in the parlor: Elizabeth and Bill, Agnes, Beatrice and Candace, and Paulina. The Emersons were there, Elliott and Charlotte, warming their hands and chatting with the Havershams, Mariah, and Peabody. Susan and Wesley had been given a wing of the house to call home, so they were there too, helping with things to drink and generally being hospitable. (Dr. Brown had left town that morning to tend some ailing orchids in Cedarville.) Firelight from the big fireplace was reflected in the glass balls decorating a Christmas tree that stretched pine-scented boughs all the way to the ceiling.

Lady Lydia, with some help, handed them glasses of punch and plates of tiny, delicious treats. More mugs of hot chocolate appeared. Elizabeth heard music, and when she leaned into the adjoining room, she saw Professor Longley at the piano, his coat tails splayed out over the bench and trailing majestically across the floor behind him. He smiled and beckoned. Before she could quite tell how it happened, she had joined him on the piano bench, and everyone gathered round to sing Christmas carols. Sir Wallace gestured to divide them into groups that sang counterparts and harmonies, and when Charlotte sang "Good King Applesauce," instead of "Wenceslas," Elizabeth got the giggles, and Elliott Emerson had to grab her, so she didn't fall off the bench.

Then Lady Lydia offered to show everyone around the house, all the rooms, staircases and porches and balconies. By the time they returned to the foyer, dinner was served. China and crystal sparkled under candlelight, platters of roast beef and bowls of mashed potatoes rubbed elbows with round casseroles full of buttery carrots and heaps of fluffy dinner rolls.

Glittering dishes of candied cranberries sat beside bubbling bowls of corn pudding. Even the spinach salad looked festive, dark green leaves glistening under a glaze of oil and bacon pieces. It was a feast.

Afterwards, helpers brought out steaming apple pies with sugar crystals on their delectable brown crusts, and side dishes of ice cream to scoop over the top. It was hard to choose between the pie and the four-layer chocolate cake, but there was enough for guests to have as much as they cared to have. Elizabeth felt up to trying both and did. She felt eager and excited in the festive atmosphere and found herself chattering to Susan. She did not know, but for the first time since she had arrived in Granger's Green, she was acting like someone who was ten years old, not a ten-year-old grownup.

Sir Wallace, at the head of the table, rose and clinked his glass to gain their attention. "We are here because of the brave deeds of one young lady," he said. "Elizabeth, I'm glad to see your beautiful new dress. I have good news, and mysteries to explain. After which, we'll have more music and…presents?" He glanced at Peabody, who nodded.

He continued. "Your arrival in Granger's Green, Elizabeth, stirred up questions that demanded answers. Why would girls have to run away from the orphanage Lydia and I set up as a haven?"

Charlotte Emerson remarked, seriously, "E-liz-a-bet *escaped* me!" Her father *shooshed* her, but Sir Wallace just smiled.

"Elizabeth, what happened to your parents? Where did that baby ring that matches Lydia's come from? Why did Cook take you under her wing?"

Charlotte frowned. "Cook has *wings?*" and several people found quick ways to hide a chuckle.

"With concern about Simon Suggs, and the knowledge of that ring, Lydia and I headed to St. Gumbert's. We received a great deal of help from Cook. She told me about things that happened eleven, almost twelve, years ago."

Lady Lydia jumped into the discussion. She seemed barely able to contain her excitement: "Wallace found a birth certificate for a baby girl, born almost eleven years ago on the third floor of St. Gumbert's! That baby girl was *Elizabeth,* and that baby girl's mother is *right here!*"

There were gasps. Elizabeth looked around. "My...mother?" she whispered.

Sir Wallace proceeded carefully. "Cook showed me the orphanage files and showed me a birth certificate she said was yours. Then I went to the hospital where they sent your mother, expecting nothing more than to find a record of her death. But the hospital records were clear. Your mother had been there for a very long time, recovering from a fever that erased her memory."

Lady Lydia took up the tale. "And as I was starting to say, back at the orphanage—the hospital records showed that this patient, who arrived at St. Gumbert's because she had every right to call it home, because she expected to be cared for there when she had her baby, because the place rightfully *belonged* to her. The lady is Elizabeth's mother."

Sir Wallace extended his arm toward Susan.

Elizabeth concentrated on catching every word. She looked at Susan Haversham, who looked back and nodded.

"When I ran away from Wesley, I didn't know I was going to have a baby. You. The details of everything that happened in those difficult years are only starting to come back to me.

"My mother told me all about the Granville mansion. She had lived there when she was little. She called it our family home. So, after the argument with Wesley, it seemed like the best place to go. Cook took me in, and I worked with her in the kitchen for several years. I'm just beginning to remember."

Wesley cleared his throat and patted Susan's hand. "Elizabeth—you are our daughter."

Charlotte clapped her hands and exclaimed "E-liz-a-bet has a *daddy!*"

Deep inside, Elizabeth was not shocked. Wesley's words had given voice to something she'd known all along, without knowing she knew. Her question, "My father?" was a request for an explanation, which Wesley provided.

"I never knew you existed. Susan ran away to St. Gumbert's. I was traveling the countryside and couldn't be found. Susan got very sick and lost her memory."

Sir Wallace added some details. "You should have been treated royally, Susan. Because the St. Gumbert's mansion belongs to your family, you and our Elizabeth are the last of the Granvilles."

"When Matron heard your mother's story," continued Lady Lydia, "she saw the two of you as a threat. That's when things started to go very wrong at the orphanage, about ten years ago. Matron built the wall, moved the orphans into the dormitory, and started to steal. She wanted to steal that baby ring the minute she saw it, Cook told me. Because it came with the lady who had the baby, the lady who could take over the whole asylum, because, even though she didn't know, the whole place belonged to her. Matron would have confiscated the ring—but Cook stopped her. Once she took sick..."

"—Mehitabel the cook," continued Sir Wallace, "kept the ring until Elizabeth was old enough to take care of it. And she kept an eye on you, too," he said, looking at Elizabeth, "after your mama was sent off to the hospital. She brought you into the kitchen where she could protect you. She's not a very good cook, Elizabeth, but she did the best she could. You know, when the orphans were served those good gypsy stews for dinner, Cook paid for them with her own money."

"The Matron should have written to us the instant you were put in her care," said Lady Lydia, angry red spots showing on her cheeks. "Even though we were traveling. Heavens, the object of our travels was to find

Susan! But she hid the information. She did not want St. Gumbert's' rightful owner around. When you arrived in Granger's Green, of course Hepzibah Sharpe knew who you were, because her sister had called her."

"And my mother"—Elizabeth looked at Susan a little shyly—"was upstairs in her house?"

"That's right. When Hepzibah tried to trap you in that pointy, prickly front room, your own mother was upstairs in the tower, where she had been imprisoned for years. And when she started speaking, and singing...her words jammed up Dr. Brown's and Peabody's systems something fierce. And then," Lady Lydia paused for breath, "*you* came to town, and the system couldn't separate your words from those of your own mother."

"The problem wasn't that you didn't belong, but that you both belonged," said Peabody.

Sir Wallace added, "I think the whole orphanage scheme was Hepzibah's idea. Winifred Sharpe—Matron—does not have the brains or the gumption to devise such a plan. I think Winifred actually believed Susan died in that hospital."

He continued: "Hepzibah saw the orphanage as a way to make money, and Winifred, I'm afraid, went along with her. Hepzibah never told her Susan was here in Granger's Green, and Winifred never visited."

Lady Lydia added, "Their sisters Letitia—Mrs. Short—and Mehitabel—Cook—knew nothing about the thievery and not much about the deception. But Lettie Short was bitter. She couldn't help but notice that her sister Hepzibah always had plenty of money, while she never had enough."

Elizabeth wondered if anyone else in the room felt like the world had spun around, and what had been "down" an hour ago was now "up." She felt dizzy, so she sat very still. The rustle of Susan's blue cloak on one side, the tweed of Wesley's best jacket on the other, were reassuring, and gave her a sense of balance, of being at home.

"There's a special room here for you, and a place in our hearts," Susan whispered.

Elizabeth experienced a warm feeling of belonging.

Phineas Peabody handed out Christmas gifts from his battered red satchel. Each person received a mechanical sculpture made from pieces of brass fittings and couplings, from down in the Feathergill's basement. Elizabeth's was a silver cat, made from silver rings and gears and tiny pipes, with a head that bobbed because it was mounted on a spring. She loved it immediately.

# Epilogue

This adventure is almost over. The Great St. Gumbert's Scandal was a big story in the Gumbertville newspaper well into the new year, as girls who had been kidnapped were given back to joyful families, and longsuffering tradesmen finally were paid. Paulina was the reporter who wrote the story, and her excellent work landed her a newspaper job that she holds to this day.

Townspeople, eager to take tours of the Granville Mansion (the building's original name) could do so because the first thing done was the demolition of the hideous wall surrounding it.

Phineas Peabody went there on a temporary assignment. He set up shop in the basement, with Dr. Brown for help. The precious Feathergill's plans were retrieved from the wreck of Simon Suggs's car, and were used to begin a word-plant at the orphanage.

That spring, a group from Granger's Green took the train to Gumbertville to see the changes and improvements. After Peabody gave them a tour of the cellars, they settled in a big parlor, where spring sunshine flooded the room. The chairs and sofas were filled with Sir Wallace and Lady Lydia, Wesley and Susan, Dorrie and Tony, Elizabeth, Mariah, and Peabody, who sat on a hard chair and fiddled with an oilcan hanging from his pocket loop. Dr. Brown had been staying in an upstairs chamber, and he joined them, rubbing sleep from his eyes.

Lady Lydia was eager to tell of new developments. "When Wallace and I were here in December," she began, "I had an idea. I wanted to spin all that word-dust from St. Gumbert's halls and attics into beautiful new clothes for the orphans. I called Peabody. He told me he couldn't, because the dust belonged to girls who'd long since grown up and moved away. I saw his point.

"But together, we had another idea. All that historic word dust could surely be made into something beautiful! Peabody, brilliant engineer that he is, took the first train out after Christmas, and set to work."

Elizabeth thought she heard him say "shucks" under his breath as he undid the clasp of his ancient red satchel. Reaching in, he pulled out a skein of thread, twisted into a figure eight. Elizabeth, sitting next to him, could see the glittery thread was thick and strong.

"I've always said Granger's Green was up ahead of every other town. But over here, I thought more could be done with words even than we've been manufacturatin' there. Words could be more than clothes. Wesley was proof of that, under our own noses! We can build amazin' things with words, I started thinkin'.

"What I'm presentin'," Phineas waved the skein of thread, "is the stuff comin' out of the new process estabbled here. We got the word-plants growin'," —he nodded at Dr. Brown—"then got machinery up and runnin', and up and runnin' it is. I got Tony and Vera Louise, and Willemina, two of

250

those bright girls here, trained on how things work and what to do if things go wrong.

"We took the wheels off of Tony's gypsy cart, and turned 'em into big spinning wheels. He and Miss Dorrie are going to get matri-fied" — Elizabeth translated this into 'married' — "so they don't need a travelin' cart. They're gonna stay on and take care of the orphanage. Right handy, sensible people."

Susan took Peabody's thread in her hands. "This is the kind of fiber that makes brocade," she said.

"Yes'm. And no amount of tweaking or coaxing could make those words be anything soft or light. They're solid things that spin into fabric that'll last for centuries. What we saw comin' off the loom started formin' pitchers!" Elizabeth automatically translated "pitchers" into "pictures."

"And then, more pitchers! Right before our eyes, pitchers made of words stored up all those years in the attics and the bedrooms and the cellars of this big house. Turns out, old words act different from new ones. Stands to reason. Miss Dorrie and Mr. Tony, and the girls, we just stood silent-like and watched the words form the pitchers."

"Phineas, you're a genius," said Sir Wallace.

Peabody smiled.

"Pictures of *what?*" Susan asked.

Peabody reached into his satchel and handed out pieces of woven cloth. When he had gone around the room, each person had a tiny tapestry with the first letter of their name woven in. Mariah's "M" was decorated with a needle and thread, Charlotte's "C" with a pencil. Elizabeth's "E" featured, to her astonishment, a glittering crown worked into the design.

"These small samplers are tiny prophecies, and they are just the beginning, I think we'll have exquisite tapestries when all the words have worked their way through your system, Phineas." Sir Wallace smiled. "And," he added, sensing the question in Elizabeth's mind, "Peabody and

Dr. Brown have put together a basement plant-and-pipe system to catch the orphans' words and make them their own clothes."

"That's not all!" Phineas Peabody had more to say. "I'm seein', clear as clear, that we could make much more than clothes with solid words like we gets when people think before they get to speakin'. So I set up some machinery of my own inventin', and I'm thinkin' we're gonna see building blocks and machine parts and other such matriculations" — Elizabeth had no interpretation for this—"comin' out of my inventions. St. Gumbert's could be a place for smart girls here to make things and discover things and help whatever needs helpin'." Peabody sat down.

So that's how what used to be known as St. Gumbert's Orphan Asylum became, instead, Granville's Academy of Excellence, a haven for young ladies who had no home, and a school where any girl could develop her potential and promise.

Back in Granger's Green, Letitia Short stopped almost all her complaining and found life got very much better. This surprised her. She moved into Sharpe Corners, recently vacated by her sister's imprisonment, and proved to be a better boss, Elsie the maid reported, although that is not saying much. Meanwhile, Mehitabel Sharpe—Cook—stopped cooking and took to traveling with the gypsies. She shared Poppy's cart and acquired a box of paints. Together, they traveled the countryside, with Cook painting landscape scenes she sold to shops. When the weather got cold, she kept her sister Lettie company at Sharpe Corners. They didn't argue nearly as much as you might expect two Sharpes to argue. The other two Sharpe sisters were not seen again in Granger's Green, due to the long prison sentences they received once the orphanage account books were retrieved from the wreckage of Simon Suggs's car. (Because Simon Suggs was in jail, Fred Wallerton was allowed to salvage the automobile. Being mechanically minded, he did the necessary repairs and fulfilled his dream of owning a motorcar.)

And as for Simon and Malice Suggs...well, they were able to continue operating a garment factory, of sorts, in the Gumbertville jail, where they were put to work making prison uniforms. At the time of this writing, they can be found in the prison sweatshop, spinning out scratchy, boxy garments from the same spun thistle fiber they once used at the S.U.G. factory. Hepzibah and Winifred Sharpe work there, too.

Feathergill's Emporium continues to supply citizens of Granger's Green with the garments they need, in unique fabrics and patterns and styles. Peabody trained Bill, who will no doubt be the next king in the basement empire. Mariah and Elliott Emerson seem to be sweet on each other, and we have high hopes they will make a whole family for Charlotte.

As for Elizabeth—for after all, this is her story—she found her perfect home in Granger's Green, with her parents and MacTavish and a puppy they adopted. Their home is in the Haversham mansion, and she is always welcome at Feathergill's Fabulous Emporium.

The work of the shop goes on, making everyone in Granger's Green aware of the power of their words to change their lives.

*The End*

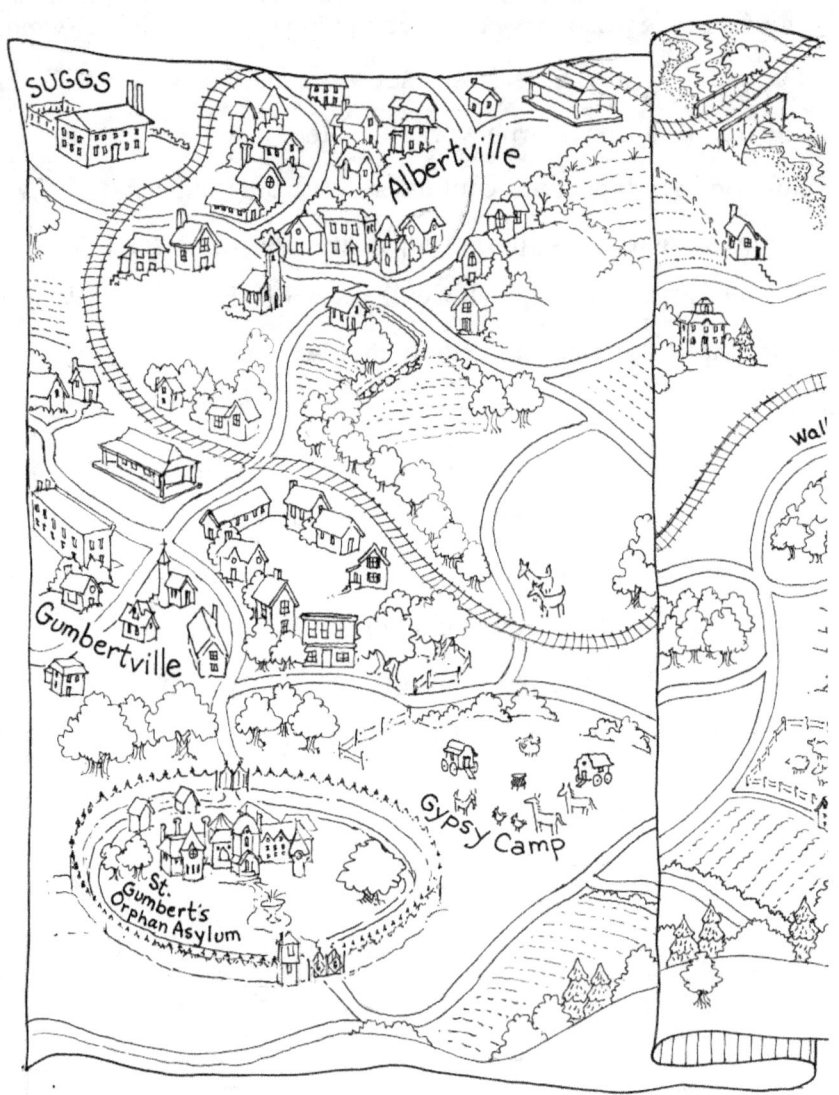

www.ingramcontent.com/pod-product-compliance
Lightning Source LLC
Chambersburg PA
CBHW082058090726
47909CB00011B/3076